Tiernan's Punishment

by

Faith V. Smith

Tiernan's Punishment

Cover Art by *Debbie Taylor*

The Wild Rose Press, Inc.
PO Box 708
Adams Basin, NY 14410-0708
Visit us at www.thewildrosepress.com

Publishing History
First Faery Rose Edition, 2013
Digital ISBN 978-1-61217-973-5
Print ISBN 978-1-62830-288-2

Published in the United States of America

"No, please, do not cut my hair."

Mista stood frozen in place, holding a strand of his moonbeam hair. Not only because of the man's muscular thighs pressed against her legs, but the almost plea in his tone touched her.

"'Tis the law to do so." Her words were a whisper of air.

"Not where I come from. To cut my hair is to unman me as a warrior." His words were guttural, but she felt the desperation in them.

"If I allow you to wear your hair long, then others will fight to keep theirs. What reason can you give me to placate my men?" She held her breath waiting for his answer.

"I am not what I seem to you. I come from a place so far away you would have to travel through what you call Midegarde to find it."

Mista wasn't prone to believe in Norse gods, although a good many of her people did so, yet she didn't correct the warrior. His eyes glowed with blue fire when he continued.

"A place where magick is commonplace, where there are no wars or...not usually." He chuckled just a bit, the sound warming Mista's heart.

"And just how did you get from there to here?" She knew she sounded scornful, but the blue-eyed charmer told a whopping tale.

"I traveled through time."

Praise for Faith V. Smith

"*TIERNAN'S PUNISHMENT* is a fast, fun read that starts with a bang and doesn't let you go. I loved the fae world, the Norse mythology, and sizzling sensuality. You can't go wrong with this paranormal read."

~Sharon Buchbinder, author of Obsession

"Again, Faith Smith has wowed me... *GIDEON'S HEART* is an intricate love tale of the purest form."

~Angela, Nocturne Romance Reads (5 Hoots)

"Readers will love the latest novel, *SEMPER FI MAGIC*, by Smith. Full of laughter and passion."

~Sabrina Cooper, Romantic Times (4.5 Stars)

"Sexy, dark, and irresistible. *DUNBAR'S CURSE* blends danger and scorching passion into a fast-paced, wicked hot story."

~Sue-Ellen Welfonder, USA Today bestselling author

"When reading this story [*VIKING, GO HOME*] this reviewer couldn't help but think of another excellent time travel, Jude Deveraux's *A Knight in Shining Armor*."

~Cindy Himler, Romantic Times (4 Stars)

"*KENSINGTON'S SOUL* is a wonderfully written, tender and thoroughly enjoyable book."

~Eaim, Night Owl Reviews (5 Stars)

"*BEWARE WHAT YOU WISH*…Time Travel fans take note of this short, sassy, sexy and highly entertaining debut by an author to watch."

~Kathe Robin

"*IMMORTAL JUSTICE* is a truly magnificent dark story of a hot steamy page-turning romance, with endless suspense!!"

~Romance Writers Reviews (5 stars)

Dedication

As always to my darling angel husband, Rick,
and my beautiful and talented daughter Amanda.

~

A special thank you to my editor, Sarah Hansen,
and to God be the glory.

Acknowledgements

To Debbie Taylor who took my idea and made it a reality with the reach out and touch cover she did for Tiernan's Punishment. Thank you from the bottom of my heart!

I would like to take a moment and thank all my readers. You have been so faithful in waiting for my next book. I am truly sorry it has taken me this long to deliver what you asked for. Now, with my back on the mend and God blessing my imagination, I hope to keep you all entertained with many more books in the future!

Special thanks for their patience in waiting go to Maryln, April, Crystal, Aislinn, Amy, Sandi, Jen, Nora, Eliza, Gini, Sharon, and Alex. I know there are more that I need to thank but please know you all are in my heart and prayers!

Chapter One

The Seelie Court

Tiernan took a sip of ambrosia mixed with whiskey and immediately set the glass down. It tasted like ashes. His gaze perused the back gardens of the castle. The rolling landscape, dotted with iridescent lights, held the remnants of his daughter's wedding. A union he'd blessed but one that could earn him a bit of trouble. When his new son-in-law asked if members of the court would punish Catriona for bringing a mortal to their world and then compounding her sins by marrying him, Tiernan had told him no. What he'd not disclosed was the fact he'd bartered himself in her place.

Now he waited for his peers as well as friends from the Fae council to arrive and pronounce his sentence. Shimmers of color twisted across the horizon. It wouldn't be much longer. Soon he would know the council's ruling and his punishment.

Tiernan embraced his royal lineage and stood straighter with his shoulders back and eyes forward. Shame at being called to task overshadowed his spirit, but he would not allow the emotion to show. His daughter deserved a chance at happiness and love—a love like he'd shared with her mother Alisanne for many millennia before she'd passed away. As for the slight hint of apprehension riding his spine, he tossed if off. After all, what could the royal council do to their king?

The council was made up of four members, in addition to Tiernan. Each served as a guardian for different realms of the Fae world. For the most part they were fair and just when it came to those who broke the law. Tiernan had handpicked three of them himself after becoming king.

Alex, Jared, and Gideon were all married to women they loved, and together they would control Willamina—the only Fae guardian that might harbor ill will toward Tiernan. The council was there to aid him, although Willamina had proven to be obstinate on more than one occasion. He'd inherited her as the only guardian left from the previous king's rule.

He shrugged his shoulders. She was not to be trusted; he and most of the male fae considered her to be a piranha when it came to the male species.

The mingled colors he'd glimpsed earlier spun into the courtyard but formed into only one figure.

Willamina struck a pose for effect. The woman's flair for dramatics and bid for attention were not welcome.

Where were the rest of the members? Against his better judgment he tried a slight smile. Perhaps he could keep matters congenial until the rest of the group arrived.

The fae smiled back. Diamond crescents twinkled among long locks of raven hair that fell almost to her waist. The crimson gown she wore hugged her curves and would have been enticing if worn by someone else. Tiernan could not summon even a remote bit of admiration for the wily fae. She'd been a thorn in his side ever since he'd rejected her blatant moves to seduce him. And that had been while he was still mated to Alisanne.

Her green eyes flashed as she walked toward him, her hips swaying to only a tune Willamina could hear.

"So Tiernan, are you ready for your verdict?" She moistened her red lips with the tip of her tongue.

"Of course, Willamina, but I'd prefer to wait on the rest of the council."

"I'm sorry, I'm bad." She reached out and caressed his bare arm. For his sentencing, he'd elected to wear a dressed-down version of his royal clothing. A black vest with the purple-and-gold armbands of his station, black leather pants and boots, as well as the circlet he preferred for a crown.

"No one else is coming." Her laugh was vicious as she raised a hand with red-tipped nails. "I'll be handing out your punishment."

Tiernan didn't like where this was going. No telling what Willamina had planned for him, but he'd survive. After all she could only do so much to him. He moved several feet away—her touch sickened him.

As he watched her green eyes began to glow with an unworldly gleam and a silver orb materialized in her outstretched hand.

Chills attacked his spine. Somehow the witch had gotten a hold of the only thing that could strike fear in his heart other than losing his precious daughters. The orb of judgment glowed with a metallic fire, and should only be used when all four members were together. As the oldest male beside Tiernan, Alex always kept the orb locked away until needed.

"How did you get the Judgment Orb? And what did

you do with the rest of the council members?"

Willamina's laughter sounded like dragon claws scraping against metal. "I did not harm them, if that's what you mean." She held up her hand and looked at her nails. "Of course, they probably won't be too happy. But that's my problem, not yours."

"What do you mean? And again, how did you get the orb from Alex?"

"Oh, that was easy. Once I put all the members and their families into a deep sleep, I took the key to the orb's cabinet." Again she laughed. "Like stealing magick from a young fae."

"Willamina, you are in violation of our court code. Other than myself, only Alex is authorized to use the Judgment Orb. If I were not available it would fall to the eldest bearing my blood. You know this." So incensed he wanted to strangle her, Tiernan battled back his rage. If he laid a hand on her in anger, he would also have to answer to that charge.

"Oh unicorn horns, Tiernan. Of course I know this, but I don't care. I've planned your downfall for a very long time, and now it's at hand."

Willamina tossed the orb from hand to hand and gave him a look that froze the marrow in his bones.

"Tiernan, King of the Seelie Court, it is your punishment to be banned from the land of the fae for a period of one year."

He relaxed just a bit. Being banned wasn't the awful sentencing he'd been afraid of—

"To the past when Vikings roamed the earth in search of humans to slay." Willamina's gaze danced with glee.

Vikings he could handle; he'd just zap—

"And for that period of time you are forbidden to use your magick." Willamina positively gloated after making her announcement.

Tiernan wanted to blast her with that same magick, and send her careening into oblivion. He raised his hand to do just that but Willamina's laughter rocked the air.

"I wouldn't try it if I were you, Tiernan. If you use your magick then you will lose it forever.

"You are not worthy of being fae, Willamina. You're a vicious witch." Tiernan stalked toward her.

"Well, you don't have to be ugly." Her eyes flashed jade and then hardened. "Your sentence has been handed out, and the orb has already been activated." She laughed again. The grating sound made him want to cover his ears.

"Why, Willamina?" His question was a ragged sensation of sound as he felt the first effects of the magick she'd put into place.

"Why not? With you out of the way and stuck in a remote area of Norway, anything could happen to you. Then I will be happy to take over as Queen of the Seelie Court."

Tiernan's horror grew. The only way she could do that was to get rid of his heirs. Could she be that cold, that evil?

"Surely you would not harm my daughters even to serve your own greed?" Spears of pain shot through his body—not all them due to magick.

"Of course not, that would mean a death sentence for me. However, I will, after a suitable amount of time, point out to the council that I would be a better ruler." She ran a hand through her hair before speaking again.

"That you are too soft when it comes to mortals,

and that we need someone who will make sure no one else brings a mortal to our world."

"Mortals are not evil—or at least not all of them, Willamina."

"I don't care. They're slimy, mealy mouthed, and they express horrible sounds from their bodies." She shuddered and then opened her mouth once more. "And just in case you think you can use your magick and then beg the council to give your powers back, I've added a codicil to the judgment."

Tiernan's insides burned with fire almost making it impossible for him to speak. "And just what would that be, witch?"

Her eyes flashed again—green ice this time. "Try using any magick at all and you will also lose your ability to bed a woman."

Before he could wrap his mind around that horrific possibility, his body lifted into the air and then rocketed downward in a spiraling rush of speed. Lights flashed in front and around him as Tiernan continued to be hurled toward an unknown destiny.

Nothing he did stopped the pain or his fall into oblivion. His eyes rolled back in his head, his body went limp, and he hit his destination like a meteor ripped out of the heavens to be flung to earth.

Blackness consumed him and Tiernan welcomed the relief.

****

894, Norseland

"Chieftain, Jarl Runolfsson's forces have passed the fjord." The thunderous shout bounced into the small room.

Mista Einarsson looked up as Baldr, her second-in-command, ran into her private sitting room.

"Should I have our warriors mount up?" The tall and bearded blond-haired Viking stood at attention, but his demeanor was anything but calm.

"Yes, thank you, Baldr. I will be right with you." Mista laid aside the book her da had given her on the rules of being a chieftain. No matter how many times she read it, she found herself picking it up at least once a sennight. Just holding the pages her da had composed made him seem closer than the halls of Valhalla where he'd wanted to go when he died. She, however, just prayed he'd made it to the gates of the Christian God. A God a group of traveling priests had told her about.

Baldr left the room quickly, and Mista headed for her chamber. Gunhilde, once one of the clan's most fearless female warriors, now married to Baldr, stood waiting. No doubt, she had also heard her husband's announcement.

"Here, mistress." Gunhilde held up a pair of leather leggings and a shirt of chain mail. The links of metal were not as heavy as what her warriors wore but would protect Mista from attack, providing no one shot an arrow between the links and if she avoided blows from a battle-ax.

"Thank you, Gunhilde." Mista knew she had at least an hour, even if the marauders rode their mounts hard, before Erik Runolfsson reached the outskirts of their village. She planned to stop him before he got that far.

She stripped off her over-gown and under-dress before pulling on the leggings. Mista raised her arms so Gunhilde could drop a cloth shirt over her head followed by the chain mail. She stood for a moment, allowing the weight to settle onto her body, before moving to her weapons chest. After retrieving a battle-ax, a broadsword, and a dagger, she strapped the blades to a leather belt Gunhilde buckled at her waist, before slamming her feet into leather boots that crawled to her knees. The last to go on was the silver helmet with a nose guard. The blacksmith of the village had made it especially for Mista.

"Blóð ok sigr," Gunhilde uttered as she grasped Mista's arm in a warrior grip.

"Aye, blood and victory." Mista prayed the blood loss would be on the side of the Runolfsson forces. Erik had no right to try and force a marriage on her. She had stood as chieftain to her people for years without taking on a mate, and she did not plan to change her status now.

Mista hoisted her shield. Her stride as she exited the hall was firm, not rushed, but determined. She would see victory today and Erik, dubbed "Long-sword" because of his sexual prowess, could take a leap in the fjord.

"Mount up," she told the warriors holding the reins of their impatient horses. The village of Einarsson stood inland, the nearest waterway the fjord Erik had just crossed. The icy blue channel, two days from the coast, meandered across several chieftain holdings, the Runolfsson Clan being one of largest next to Mista's. In order to access her lands, Erik crossed the fjord where both their properties were divided by the clear blue water, and then it was a straight line to her village.

Mista vaulted onto her horse and waved her hand. The battle cry "Einarsson!" left her lips in a shout to be echoed by fifty additional voices. She and her men rode hard and fast toward a copse of Spruce trees near the edge of her property line. It had and with God's grace would again lend its leafy bowers as a perfect place to defend her people.

She knew with certainty that if Erik scored today's victory, she and the village of Einarsson would be under his control until Mista agreed to marry him. And even then he would not allow her to carry on as chieftain of her clan. She would die before she allowed that to happen.

Erik was mean, spiteful, and an oaf of a leader. His own people turned away from him in fear when he walked through their village. His father, Dag Runolfsson, had been the same way. The man had buried at least five wives before the last one who delivered Erik and then died a short year after his birth. Dag raised his son in the same malevolent manner he lived, and the young motherless child had grown into an entity of cruelty.

His envy of her being a chieftain while he was a jarl set like a rotting pot of Lute fish. He could not understand how she'd inherited the role of leader of her clan as well as the higher rank.

Mista prodded Hauk, the warhorse her da had gifted her with several birthdays ago. The magnificent beast stretched his long limbs and did as she asked. The speed was incredible, almost as exhilarating as standing on the stern of one of her family's longboats, which were presently dry-docked until spring. The thick layers of ice coating the fjord had eased Erik's crossing onto Einarsson land. He probably reasoned he would surprise Mista, but she'd learned from the best. Posting lookouts at the four corners of Einarsson land was well worth the effort in forestalling attacks.

"My chieftain."

"Yes, Baldr." Her next-in-command didn't look at all pleased.

He leaned in nearer before speaking. "Erik will be fired up to do as much harm as possible in order to acquire your promise to marry him. 'Twould be best if you allowed *us* to draw his men into battle."

Mista eyed the man riding at her side. He'd been a dear friend of her da's and had taught her the fine art of battle when her da was gone on chieftain business, raids, and trips to sell furs. She knew Baldr meant well, but to allow her fellow clansmen to protect her like she was a weak female did not suit Mista. She would continue to prove herself worthy of keeping the chieftainship. One errant whisper in their king's ear, and she could lose all she loved.

"Nay, I cannot hide behind you or our men. And"—she kept his gaze as she continued—"you would not have it any other way."

Baldr bowed his head for a moment before sending her a brief smile. "As you wish, my chieftain."

She returned his glimmer of affection with a smile of her own. A scant few minutes later, they were at the ambush point, and a few moments after she heard the thundering sound of hooves.

Erik Runolfsson's forces were near. Time to ready for battle.

A group of men equal in number to the Einarsson warriors rounded the bend and moved into the leafy trap Mista planned to spring. A quick glance assured her that her men were ready. They awaited only one thing.

She gave it to them.

"Blóð ok sigr."

The Einarsson family motto hit the air at the same time Erik's men spotted Mista and her warriors. Their horses neighed as they were pulled roughly to a halt only to be urged forward into battle.

Mista pulled her battle-ax from its resting place at her side, and gripped her shield with her other hand. She blocked a blow from a sword and then buried the blade in her opponent's chest. Blood sprayed hot against her face, but she ignored the metallic taste and blinked to clear the crimson drops from her eyes. A quick pull and push and the warrior hit the ground.

All around friend and enemy alike slashed and hacked at one another. She hated this aspect of being chieftain. After every battle a morass of guilt consumed her because someone had died. Yet, to not fight would make her and her clansmen victims of a stronger adversary.

The melee grew fierce. Mista fought off two more warriors before Erik reached her side. She lifted her weapon and planned to skewer him in half. Before she could, from out of nowhere a beam of light cut through the shadows of the copse, blinding Mista with its intensity. When her vision returned to normal, she barely had time to bring her shield up before Erik Long-sword brought his battle-ax down in an arc toward her head.

Chapter Two

Tiernan came back to consciousness with a groan. His head roared with pain, his body throbbed with a sundry of aches, and his vision came and went so he closed his eyes.

He gently eased trembling hands to his abused head, before rapidly transferring them to his ears when a thunderous, clanging, horrific din assaulted them.

He would kill Willamina when his sentence was up. The fae-witch deserved the most dismal punishment Tiernan could devise. In the meantime, he dragged his eyelids open once more, sat up, and looked around.

The landscape before him was a frigid nightmare of iced branches, snow-covered ground, and a battle royal. Whether by design or accident, Willamina had managed to drop him, if Tiernan wasn't mistaken, right in the midst of a battle between two opposing forces.

The combatants left a path of blood and severed limbs as they crept closer to him. He ran his hands down his naked arms in an effort to get his blood pumping again. His armbands felt like hunks of iced metal. His circlet was missing, probably lost in the tunnel of torture that flung him to earth. He should have foregone his chosen outfit for something warmer. With his magick at stake, he could not use it to regulate his body temperature, and if he didn't get warm soon, he would be dead from hypothermia—if a sword didn't slice him in half first.

Tiernan staggered to his feet and almost fell when a warhorse danced into his line of sight. The warrior on its back looked crazed with blood lust. His chain mail was covered in blood and other body fluids. Tiernan dodged out of the Viking's way and dove for a tangle of bushes.

He dared anyone to call him a coward. The fact being, he had never run from a battle before. But he'd always been able to defend himself either with a weapon or magick.

His death would only result in chaos at the Seelie Court, and cause his daughters, especially Catriona, heartache and misery. Catriona would have to fight Willamina for the throne, and the fact she was married to a mortal would only hurt any case she brought before the council.

The chill in his bones grew worse, and it was all he could do keep his teeth from chattering. He needed to concentrate. He needed a weapon, and then he needed to get the *Fae* away from this battle. What he knew about Norse history could be put on one KB of a memory stick. Yet, what Tiernan did know was when in battle most Viking warriors could go berserk. Something he didn't plan to wait around to see.

He needed to survive and then find a place he could stay until he would be free to go home.

The battle escalated around him. A severed hand attached to a small knife flew through the air and landed at his feet. A dead body followed. The aforementioned warrior rode off.

Tiernan ignored the gore coating the blade's shaft and pried the mangled man's fingers open. He could use the weapon, as well as the chain mail the Viking wore.

The metal shirt abraded his bare arms and carried the chill of the air within its links. Still, it helped block some of the wind that had suddenly sprung up. Tiernan decided not to pry the helmet off the warrior's head, instead he hastily moved away from the sound of battle.

His bid for safety stalled when a warrior on foot accosted him. Tiernan cursed. Too many fortnights had passed since he'd wielded a weapon of any kind, and the dagger he'd confiscated would be no match for a battle-ax.

The decision to die or run was fought and won in less than a second. Tiernan threw the knife at the man's nose-plate and waited. The instinct to use his magick was hard to control, but he won the fight—barely. One moment the warrior stood there, the next he hit the snow-covered ground with a thud. The blade buried to the hilt in the Viking's left eye.

Whether luck or skill, Tiernan's path to freedom lay ahead, away from the warriors and their bloodlust. Relieved he took two steps before the horizon around him darkened, and his eyes rolled back in his head.

****

Mista ignored Erik's scare tactics. She knew he would not kill her. If he did he would never get her land. She had already named Baldr as her successor in the event of her death if she wasn't wed first.

"Leave off, Erik. This fight is old and unwelcome, just as your overbearing suit is." Mista spat the words and watched Runolfsson's face turn an ugly shade of red.

"Stubborn bitch. You have no right to those lands.

They should have been deeded to me," he snarled back.

"Why? Because you're a man? I'm sorry, but that's not of consequence to me. I am my father's daughter and chieftain of Clan Einarsson. That will not change, and you will never have control over my people." Mista moved her horse out of the way of Baldr's advancing steed as he pursued one of Erik's men.

"We will see about that, Mista. Terrible things can happen to a woman alone and even to those she holds dear." Erik looked around and saw what she did. The battle was almost over, most of his men were on the ground, or retreating like the *österkligrings* they were. She wanted no dealings with weaklings.

"Another day, Mista." Erik dropped his weapon back to his side.

"'Tis a certainty." Mista watched as he wheeled his horse around and fled like the coward he was and always had been.

Her men were gathering prisoners and seeing to the injured on both sides. She, unlike Erik, would make sure his warriors received care. It was the honorable thing to do.

Cedric, one of her youngest warriors, limped slightly as he gathered up several riderless horses. Mista scanned the area again and was pleased to see the last of Erik and Clan Runolfsson. Her sigh of relief exploded into the cold air at the same time Baldr dragged a man dressed in chain mail forward.

His lower body was covered in black leather. Long blond hair matted with blood covered the warrior's face. The one thing that struck Mista as odd was the man's lack of weapons. Had he been disarmed during the battle? And if so why was he alive? No warrior could stand up to the onslaught of such a heated battle and survive without fighting back.

"Who is he?" Mista asked, as she remained mounted.

"I do not know. I found him on the other side of those bushes. He was out cold, and there was no one else with him." Baldr dropped the wounded man to the ground. His head thudded against the hard earth, and Mista fought to keep a grimace off her lips. She should be used to the cruelty of battles, but she did not see the need to batter one already injured.

Taking prisoners was nothing new, but this one seemed different. The chain mail was too large for his frame, although his shoulders carried a warrior's build. And what was he doing in the midst of a battle with ill-fitting clothing and without a helmet?

Regardless of these unusual facts, he was a stranger on Einarsson lands. Possibly harmless, but Mista could not take a chance on leaving him behind.

"Chieftain?" Sigri, brother to Gunhilde held up a knife. "I found this near where Baldr found the warrior. It carries the markings of the Runolfsson clan."

****

Tiernan awoke for the second time with an aching head, and again he rested on the hard ground. This was getting old, and he'd had just about enough. The knives slicing through his brain had to be silenced. He began the healing spell only to stop abruptly.

Magick was forbidden. Merciful Fae, he'd almost forgotten that small fact and what it could mean for his future as king. But he would not forget that Willamina was responsible for his predicament, and she would be held accountable. Although, it wasn't unheard of for a fae to be banned for a span of time, this was ridiculous. To be tossed back into an iced nightmare without a way to defend himself from illness or physical threat was nothing but cruel.

"Bring him. We will question him later. I am curious to know how and why he was in the midst of the battle between our clan and Runolfsson's."

He heard the words from somewhere above his head, and Tiernan eased opened his eyelids. A horse's hoofs were in his immediate sight, and then his gaze traveled upward. The warrior seated on the massive stallion stared down at him.

A warrior, but not quite a warrior. The build was all wrong unless the midget holding a bloodied sword was the runt of this Viking group. He rose up and rested his body weight on his forearms. The warrior blinked, and Tiernan could have sworn the blue eyes and dark lashes hiding within the confines of the helmet were feminine in feature.

His contemplation on the warrior's gender was rudely interrupted when he was snatched to his feet, and his hands were lashed behind his back. Tiernan snarled at his captor and almost lost his footing from the barehanded clap he received on the side of his head.

"Enough, Baldr, put him on a mount and let's ride for home." Again the voice sounded more female than male. Before he could digest that train of thought, Tiernan was tossed onto the back of a horse.

"Hmmp." His exclamation was greeted with laughter by all but the warrior who seemed to be in charge. A bare moment later, his thighs gripped the sides of his mount as he alternately cursed and prayed he wouldn't fall off and break his neck before they arrived at a destination that would sure to be the equivalent of the dark side of the Seelie Court.

Chapter Three

Immediately upon entering her chamber, Mista cleaned and then replaced her weapons in their chest, unbuckled her belt, and begin tugging off her chain mail. By the time Gunhilde arrived she stood in nothing but the soft shirt she wore next to her skin. The chill of the chamber stirred goose bumps on her bare lower limbs.

"Here, mistress." She discarded the shirt and took the bed-robe Gunhilde held out, and pulled it on. Its wool had been spun until it was soft as a gosling's down. The material, dyed a rich blue, felt like bliss against her chilled body.

"Thank you, Gunhilde. I assume the preparations for our *náttmál* are underway." She moved to her clothing chest and pulled out an under-dress of red which she paired with an over-dress of dark blue.

"Yes, the night meal is almost ready. Did you wish to bathe before breaking your fast?" Gunhilde's brown eyes held an inquiry they normally did not have. The woman had mothered Mista since birth when not involved in battles, and had grown more protective and outspoken since she'd given up her warrior duties. 'Twasn't like her not to say what was on her mind. She as most of the clan was probably curious about the prisoner.

"What do you want to know?" Mista went to the

pitcher of water sitting on a plain oak table near the bed and wet a cloth. After dabbing on a bit of lye soap scented with rose petals from the past summer, she begin bathing her face, chest, and arms.

"Well, now, 'tis the usual practice to house all the prisoners in one cell in the dungeon. The pretty-boy warrior is all by himself."

Leave it to Gunhilde to light on the fact the prisoner who Baldr found last was exceptionally handsome even with the blood staining one side of his face. His eyes were a deep blue, almost silver, a color you could drown in, if she were the romantic sort—which she wasn't. His hair, a mixture of blond and silver, fell far below his shoulders. His chin was clean of any whiskers and highlighted a slight dimple.

"Mistress?"

Mista pulled herself out of the pleasant description of the so far nameless warrior.

"I know 'tis a bit strange, but something about him did not fit the rest of Runolfsson's warriors. I want to speak to him before I decide what to do with him." Mista hoped her explanation sounded plausible. She wasn't truly sure she believed it herself.

There was something about the man that made her want to find out more about him before she passed sentence.

"'Tis a thieving Runolfsson, and all you need to know, mistress." Gunhilde's words were bitter, and she had every right to feel that way. She and Baldr had lost their only son, Koll, in a raid with Erik's clan two winters past.

"I understand your feelings, but I still must rule as a chieftain. I need to know more just as my da would have." Mista rinsed her face and upper body before taking the drying cloth Gunhilde held out.

"Of course." The woman, who had been the only mother Mista knew, looked miserable. Mista finished dotting the water off her flesh and then flung the towel down.

"You have nothing to apologize for." She patted the larger woman on the back. "Now come help me dress. I am starving, and want the meal over with so I can address this matter."

****

Tiernan resisted the urge to throw off the hands tugging him into an open area filled with warriors. Much to his surprise, when calling up remembered facts on ancient Norway, the building he'd been dragged into earlier was not a longhouse made of wood, but a stone building at least three stories high. Not the normal practice of Vikings, and he couldn't help but wonder why this chieftain had gone against tradition.

The hands that held him were rough in their handling, and he regretted he could not use his magick. The taller one, the one called Baldr, would look good as a pig. In the meantime, if he had a chance, he'd still love to go one-on-one with him in a fair fight.

"On your knees." Tiernan was forced to the rush-covered floor like the lowest of underlings. He a king, subjected to the actions of those who were not fit to wipe his boots. He shook his head; his thoughts were wrong. He did not believe in one person being lesser than another. He had not ruled for millennia without being fair-minded. It was just the circumstances. Perhaps he could appeal to their chieftain.

However, a glance at the raised platform didn't

reveal a warrior. Instead his gaze locked on a woman who looked like a fae princess. Her reddish-gold hair hung long and loose. Her eyes were the deepest blue Tiernan had ever seen. Their color rivaled some of the finest jewels in his castle. Lips the color of blush and a second glimmer of color resided on cheekbones that were so finely etched they could have been formed from the wings of a faery.

Her nose held just a bit of a bend, which only enhanced her ethereal countenance. For the first time since Catriona's mother had passed away, Tiernan felt something other than a sexual attraction to a woman. He wondered whom she belonged to.

"Stand up, please." The woman waved away the protest of his guard. "'Tisn't like he's going anywhere, Baldr."

Tiernan did as the woman asked. Where was her mate, where was the chieftain of her clan?

"Who are you, and how did you come to be in the midst of a battle between our clan and Erik's clan?" Her words were soft but carried an edge of determination within them. Good. He didn't particularly care for weak women.

Now what could he tell her without being accused of being a sorcerer or a warlock? Either one would result in a watery or fiery death. Perhaps he should tell the truth or as much of it as he dared.

"My name is Tiernan. I woke up at the edge of the battle. I assure you, lady, that I am not your enemy." He knew his answer sounded ludicrous but maybe—

"If that is the case, then why were you dressed in our enemy's chain mail?"

Her question was a fair one. He only hoped he

could give her an answer that would satisfy her and the warriors.

"I borrowed the chain mail from a warrior who was already dead, and it was for protection only." He caught her gaze. Her eyes had widened, and her lips were slightly parted.

"If I choose to believe you, then how did you get here, and from where do you come?"

"I come from a land that is a long distance from here, and it was not of my choosing." Tiernan hoped for a bit of sympathy in her gaze, even pity would be helpful if she would only believe him.

"No matter how he came to be here, he bears watching. We know nothing of him or his past." Baldr's words crushed any hope he had of persuading the lady to release him.

"True." She gave Tiernan a hard stare before looking away. "

I will render judgment at the next *Thing*."

Tiernan's hope disappeared. He knew what she meant. Vikings were known to meet at certain times to decide the fate of those accused of a crime, and any squabble between clan members would also be addressed.

"Might I ask when this will be and what your chieftain will do with me in the meantime?" Tiernan kept his tone respectful. There would be no point in upsetting the lady—especially if she were the daughter or wife of the chieftain. He hoped it was the former.

"Three sennights from Thursday next. In the meantime, you will take on the duties of a thrall." The lady stood up.

A *thrall*? She would make him a slave?

"Mistress, I am most appreciative of being allowed to speak to you, but I would like a chance to present my case earlier than your monthly airing of squabbles. Perhaps to the chieftain of your clan." Tiernan waited expectantly.

The laughter began as a low rumble and then escalated until it hit every corner of the room.

What could be so amusing?

The lady halted her exit, and although her lips carried a slight tilt to them, her blue gaze held no humor.

"You have already done so. I am chieftain of the Einarsson clan."

****

Tiernan stumbled after being tossed head first into his cell. Frigid air met his body with a ferocious bite. He turned and glared at the man called Baldr.

"What are you staring at?" he growled.

The blond-haired Viking gave Tiernan an equally menacing look.

"I be not sure." The man crossed his arms and smirked. "Still, you will make a pretty thrall."

Tiernan wanted nothing more than to zap the Viking's ass into oblivion, yet he couldn't. At least not at the moment.

"I will be no man's slave." He hoped he was speaking the truth. To think otherwise would only set his temper to boil. Something he could ill afford at the present.

"We shall see, *thrall*."

Before Tiernan could stretch his arm through the bars and grasp Baldr by the neck the warrior turned and left, his chuckle falling into the chilly air of the dungeon.

Only after the last fading thuds of the man's boots trailed away did he allow his head to bow forward.

Damn Willamina. Yes, he'd broken a rule or two—though nothing as drastic as life or death, even though his son-in-law had been saved by fae magick.

Did he blame his daughter for bringing her mortal husband to the Seelie Court? No, he would have done the same to help his soul mate.

Tiernan moved to the pile of straw he assumed served as a bed. His sense of cleanliness did not allow him to investigate what vermin might be hiding within the odorous and rotting mess.

His only hope rested with sweet-talking the lovely chieftain into listening with an open mind as to why he was trespassing on Einarsson lands. And he needed to do so before he was turned into a thrall.

He gingerly stretched out on his bed and rested his head on his bent forearm. There was nothing to be done at the moment unless he ignored Willamina's warning. But Tiernan didn't want to lose his magick; without it he would not be a fit king, at least not in the fae world. His sigh stirred a piece of rotted straw as he thought about the second codicil of his sentencing. In the past he could take or leave sex, but for some strange reason the sensual beauty who held his future in her hands made him want to keep his male part in good shape.

Something about the petite warrior woman stirred him, even before she'd changed out of her chain mail. But dressed as a woman, the dark blue of her gown almost matched the azure color of her eyes. And although she looked to be fairly tall standing on the dais, he didn't think she would quite reach the center of his chest. Tiernan groaned as his shaft filled with blood.

Why was he even thinking of the woman in any way but perfecting his escape? He needed to come up with a plan of action. No way would he allow himself to be made a slave.

Once, countless millennia ago, Tiernan had been robbed of his freedom and although only for a brief span of time, he would never allow that to happen again.

He pulled his thoughts away from being a slave and tried to think of something else, only to be led back to the Einarsson chieftain. Tiernan forced his eyes to close. He needed to sleep in order to clear his mind so he would be prepared to plead his case.

****

The sound of a key being inserted into the cell door woke Tiernan. He sat up and stifled the urge to curse. He'd gotten soft living the life of a king. Every bone he had hurt, and without his magick to dispel the aches and pains he'd have to suffer as any mortal would.

"Here is a bite to break your fast, though I think 'twould be best to let you starve."

The warrior speaking wasn't the hulking Baldr, but just as distasteful to Tiernan's way of thinking. Ignoring his discomfort he jumped to his feet and moved as close to his smirking jailer as the cell door would allow.

"I assure you that I will make you suffer unspeakable horrors before I die." Whether it was the determined but calm tone he used to deliver his statement, or possibly his eyes might have begun to glow, the man blanched, shoved the cloth holding Tiernan's proposed breakfast through the opening, and backed up.

Tiernan snarled, just for the pure pleasure of knowing he could, before resuming his seat on the straw. He picked at the tough chunk of bread and moldy cheese, before forcing half of it past his unwilling lips. Digesting the unappetizing fare would serve the purpose of giving him sustenance as well as a few moments to come up with a tale that would thaw the Viking ice princess.

He tossed the remains of his meal to the rat scurrying in the corner of the cell just as the guard returned. It would only take a flick of his wrist and the man would be dead. Another flick of magick and Tiernan could be home.

His mind wavered over the delightful possibility.

"Time to go. The chieftain will be waiting."

Chapter Four

"Thor's hammer!" Mista cursed as she tripped over a pair of soft leather slippers. She was running late to oversee their captive's transformation into a thrall. The dragonflies in her belly were fighting so fiercely she hoped she would not lose the scant food she'd consumed.

Why was she so nervous? The man was nothing to her. Just an enemy she needed to deal with. But what if he was innocent? Mista shook her head and sent a wave of hair into her eyes. She'd meant to pin it up but she'd slept past her normal rising. Gunhilde's upset about the prisoner seemed to have returned. The woman had barely spoken a word when she arrived moments after Mista awakened and dropped a tray of food on the table.

To be fair, Mista understand her angst, but she had to do what was right. Until more evidence could be gathered, she would not put the man to death or even sell him on the block as many of her warriors and household wanted. Having him serve as a thrall until judgment would allow her to witness his behavior. Perhaps that would give her a key to the man himself.

She pulled on a pair of short boots over her leggings just as a bell rang somewhere in the bowels of the castle. Mista caught up her dagger and ran for the door. The thralls would be going about their chores and the warriors would be starting their morning fighting practice.

If she were lucky, Baldr would join the men and leave her to deal with the stranger. Or she could hope.

She took the stairs at a run and then grasped the side of the wall as she slipped a bit in her haste. Her breath escaped in small gasps. Mista shook her head—better to slow down than risk a broken limb. Even though she was anxious to see the warrior called Tiernan.

She arrived in the great hall just as he was escorted into the room by one of the younger warriors, Olav. Baldr was also there, and he looked none too pleased.

Displeasure also shone from the fjord blue of the prisoner's eyes, and whereas normally she could care less what a prisoner thought, especially one of Erik's men, this man touched Mista on a level she wasn't ready to explore now, or maybe not ever. It would not benefit her to think about the handsome warrior. Even if he wasn't an enemy of her people, he did not belong with her kind.

"We are ready to shear this lout of a sheep." Baldr's comment was gleeful in nature, and his eyes held a malice she'd prefer not to see.

"Thank you, Baldr. You and Olav may go to the practice field." She knew her words would not find favor.

Her second-in-command's lips twisted into a scowl, and she braced for the coming verbal assault.

"'Twould not be a good idea for you to be alone with the prisoner." Baldr's soft tone belied the look in his brown gaze that bespoke of agitation, frustration, and a bit of anger.

"I understand your concern, but tie his hands and then place him in the chair." Mista smiled at the grizzled Viking. "He will be no trouble."

"Mista…" Baldr's words trailed off as she raised an eyebrow at his usage of her given name among those not of their clan. He knew better than to address her as such when it came to chieftain matters.

"My chieftain, I plead with you to allow Olav or myself to stay." Baldr's conciliatory words held a bite.

She could reply in kind, but she truly did love Baldr, and she understood his worry, yet…

"I know 'tis not how we normally would handle this, but Baldr, I would not ask you to leave if I felt I was in any danger. And to offset your worry…" Mista held out her hand. "I have my dagger. Trust me to use it if I need to, please." She hoped her words would placate a man who had acted as advisor to her da and to her since she'd become chieftain.

Baldr scowled. "Truth, 'tis not to my liking, but I will abide by your wishes."

"Thank you, my friend." Mista smiled slightly and then gestured to the dais. "Olav, please seat the man and then secure him."

Olav did as she asked dragging Tiernan up the two steps, and pushing him down into a chair. He then took a piece of braided hemp and secured the prisoner's hands behind his back.

At a nod from Baldr, Olav left. Baldr stood his ground. "Chieftain, are you sure you would not have me stay?"

She caught his hand and patted it. "I will be fine. I was trained by two of the best Vikings that have ever been born."

Mista did not have to say who those men were; she and Baldr both knew it was him and her da.

"All right, but if this dog gives you any trouble, do not hesitate to gut him." Baldr slanted a look at Tiernan before following Olav from the hall.

Mista watched Tiernan as he watched Baldr leave. She expected the man was relieved to have her bloodthirsty mentor gone. When he finally looked up at her, she was amazed.

The man's blue eyes glinted with laughter. How was that possible? He should be frightened to death.

"I would not be amused if I were in your position."

Tiernan bit back the chuckle he wanted to release. The woman in front of him, chieftain status or not, was the size of a gnat compared to him. Even sitting down he was eye-level with her heavenly blue gaze.

And she was just as sensually alluring now, as she was last night and in his dreams. He'd love to take her to bed, to suckle the breasts she kept hidden under the loose tunic she wore, and to pull her astride his lap. The leggings encasing her lower frame would not be an impediment to feeling her lush bottom.

The thought of taking the miniature chieftain sent a pulse-wave of heat straight to his shaft. So strong was the current of lust, Tiernan prayed she would not notice.

It would just take one outraged scream to bring down the entire Einarsson clan. Something he did not relish happening.

"My apologies, Chieftain Einarsson. It was just a passing fancy." He hoped she would let it go.

"Do you not realize you are a prisoner?" Her sunset hair spun in a kaleidoscope of colors as she walked up and down the narrow strip between the table and the wall.

"I assure you, that is something I am not likely to forget." Tiernan flexed his wrists, but the rope didn't give even the width of a petite faery wing.

"Well, there is no reason to put off what needs to be done." Mista, as Baldr called her, opened a leather box, removed a metal circlet, and stepped forward.

Tiernan watched cautiously. What did the woman plan to do with the metal jewelry?

"'Twill only take a moment so hold still." She walked behind him, and he felt the cold brace of the necklace against his throat.

There was something he needed to remember about the band she'd placed against his skin, but what?

He heard an ominous click.

"What is this for?"

The woman moved to face him. "Where are you from, and why do you not know about the thrall collar?"

Tiernan's mind raged against the implications. He knew they were going to make him a slave, but he'd planned to leave long before being branded.

"Remove the collar. I will not wear it." His tone rose as the indignity and truth of his plight registered.

"You have no choice." She didn't glare at him, but her gaze was relentless in its seriousness.

"Free me. I will show you what choices I have." Tiernan's heart beat so hard he could feel the pulse inside his head. His fingers trembled at the thought of spending the next year as a slave, subject to any and all that the woman in front of him might command.

"The collar remains and will continue to stay for the length of your servitude."

"Length?" Tiernan spit out the question.

"Yes, once we meet for the *Thing*, it will be decided how long you will serve the Einarsson clan."

"This is a travesty of justice. Just because I was near a battle with your enemy, you capture me and deny my freedom." He again twisted his wrists, trying to get the unforgiving rope to loosen.

"If you are innocent of any crime then you will be freed." The Einarsson chieftain picked up the dagger and moved to stand between Tiernan's thighs.

"What are you planning now?" His growl was received with silence for a moment, but then the woman took a deep breath.

"A thrall must have his hair shorn to a certain length."

The rage that had been consuming Tiernan dissipated like sun-dried dew. The new emotion touching him was simply one of horror. Never since he'd grown into manhood had he allowed his hair to be shorter than past his shoulders. His hair was a symbol of his age and stature as a fae. Fae men who were turned out from the court even kept their hair.

He wasn't a vain man, but losing his locks as a symbol of slavery would nigh on kill him.

The fae at court would mock him, taunt him, and unmercifully brand him with their barbs.

"No, please, do not cut my hair."

Mista stood frozen in place, holding a strand of his moonbeam hair. Not only because of the man's muscular thighs pressed against her legs, but the almost plea in his tone touched her.

"'Tis the law to do so." Her words were a whisper of air.

"Not where I come from. To cut my hair is to unman me as a warrior." His words were guttural, but she felt the desperation in them.

"If I allow you to wear your hair long, then others will fight to keep theirs. What reason can you give me to placate my men?" She held her breath waiting for his answer.

"I am not what I seem to you. I come from a place so far away you would have to travel through what you call Midegarde to find it."

Mista wasn't prone to believe in Norse gods, although a good many of her people did so, yet she didn't correct the warrior. His eyes glowed with blue fire when he continued.

"A place where magick is commonplace, where there are no wars or...not usually." He chuckled just a bit, the sound warming Mista's heart.

"And just how did you get from there to here?" She knew she sounded scornful, but the blue-eyed charmer told a whopping tale.

"I traveled through time."

His words dropped into the pregnant silence, and Mista dropped the dagger—narrowly missing the man's groin and her foot before it clattered to the rush-covered floor.

"Dammit, woman, are you planning to neuter me as well as as take my hair?"

"Nay, but your words are fantasy. There is no such thing as time travel." Mista flung her statement at him as she released his hair and bent to pick up the dagger. She retrieved the weapon and straightened up, only to lose her balance. Her hands connected with the warrior's thighs, and her gaze was drawn to his manroot. She quickly removed her hands and reached once more for his hair.

"Please, I know it's hard to grasp, but what if I could prove it?"

She knew it was foolishness to believe the man, but she'd learned to judge men over the years, and his intent gaze showed no dishonesty.

"Perhaps, I would be willing to listen, but for right now I need to—"

"Then allow me to keep my hair until such a time we can talk about how I got here."

Mista was torn between duty and her instincts, and although in the past they had both been the same, this time she needed to make a choice. Besides, what harm would it do for him to keep his hair? The thought of cutting such a beautiful mane made her feel a bit sick.

"All right, but you must braid and keep it tucked inside your tunic."

The moment the words were out of Mista's mouth, Baldr walked into the hall.

"Is there a problem, mistress? You have not cut his hair." Her second-in-command smirked. "I will be glad to do the job for you."

"No, thank you, Baldr." She gave Tiernan a look that stopped the words she knew waited to spill forth.

"Our prisoner will be keeping his hair, for now." She held up her hand when Baldr looked to argue.

"See that it is braided and tucked under his tunic, and he needs something to wear to complete his chores." She turned back to Tiernan. "We will speak later on what you have told me. In the meantime, you will be put to work in the stables."

Mista stepped off the dais. "Yes, Baldr, I know 'tis

not usually done, but 'tis a man thing for his clan." She gave him a hard stare. "Surely you understand the honor involved when it comes to all things male?"

As Baldr stood there with his mouth opening and closing like a Lute fish, Mista made her escape.

Chapter Five

Tiernan resisted the urge to scratch at his wool-chafed skin. He would not give the warrior guarding him the satisfaction. After Mista left the hall, they cut the ties restricting his hands, and handed him a leather strap. He'd braided his hair and then pulled on a smelly tunic they'd tossed his way before being marched to the stables. There he'd spent the rest of the day mucking out stalls.

He didn't mind the work—he loved horses—nor did he mind the stares, jeers, and general feeling of being made fun of. His anger at his circumstances had mellowed somewhat after speaking with the sexy chieftain. Tiernan wasn't sure who was more surprised at Mista allowing him to keep his hair, Baldr or himself. Despite the mongrel's curses, he'd not said anything to Tiernan. But the man's sullen attitude didn't bode well for the future. It would be best if he could stay out of Baldr's sight.

"Pretty boy."

Thinking of the devil must have conjured up his nemesis. Tiernan stopped his scooping, and leaned nonchalantly on the handle of the shovel, an action sure to irritate Baldr. Oh well, he was bored, might as well have a bit of entertainment.

"Were you speaking to me?" His words held just the amount of sarcasm Tiernan wanted to imply.

"Aye, but you have lost some of your prettiness thanks be the gods."

"Is there a reason you do not like me or is it because you cannot claim the right to the beauty you afford me?" He knew his words were flammable but the man got on his last nerve. Yes, he was sweaty and hot—something he never thought he would be after being tossed into the frigid temp of the stable. Yes, he had dirt and probably other odorous scents on his body, but he'd given a good day's work.

"Why you little whoreson. I should break your neck and be done with the trouble I'm sure you will cause me." Baldr's words were terse, but Tiernan knew the warrior would not dare go against his mistress's orders.

"And hence the rub—you can't, and until the *Thing*, I am charged with playing slave, but that, my friend, will change." Tiernan leaned a bit closer to the man who now stood almost boot-to-boot to him.

"Think upon it this way, Baldr. You do not really know me, where I come from, or what I can truly do. One day, my not-so-friendly keeper, there will be a reckoning."

"You threaten me, slave?" Baldr reached out one of his meaty fists.

Tiernan stood his ground. Better to show the man he could not be bullied.

"Yes, but it will wait. Now, I assume you had a reason for intruding on my chores." The grin he wanted so much to display remained hidden when Baldr's face turned the red of a rose in bloom.

"Aye, you are to clean up and then Chieftain Einarsson wishes to speak with you." The Viking's words made Tiernan's pulse surge. Mista wanting to see him could mean only one thing: she wanted to talk about time travel. Despite the scowl darkening Baldr's face, he wanted to shout for joy. Just possibly he could convince her to let him go.

What he would do once he was free was something he would need to address. Even without his use of magick, he still had a fae's cunning, and he did not plan to spend the rest of his sentence in captivity or squalor.

"Well, then I guess that is what I will do." Tiernan leaned the shovel back against the stall and then moved to the barn's entrance. He stopped, looked back at the still scowling Baldr. "So where would I go to bathe?"

****

Mista wanted to pull her hair out, and Tiernan's. What had possessed her to allow him to keep his hair? It went against the code for thralls, but of course as chieftain she could bend the laws, but why had she?

Just because the man made her insides burn with a fever of need was no reason to throw away generations of stipulations. And telling Baldr she wished to speak to the prisoner only made matters worse.

Her hands trembled as she jerked out a gown and tossed it on her bed. Gunhilde was still upset and had pretty much ignored Mista all day. Now it was time to sup, but first she needed to talk to Tiernan.

What a strange name. He had not given a surname, and she wondered if perhaps he'd been born on the wrong side of marriage. Still, bastard or not, he was a fine specimen of manhood. And that was what frightened her the most. Since her da's death and becoming chieftain, Mista had been courted by several chieftains and jarls. None had made her insides pulse with heat, or her hands to tremble at just the thought of speaking to them. She'd found them to be pleasant but not husband material. She'd sent them all away but was able to keep, for the most part, the congenial relationships she enjoyed with their clans. Erik had been the only one to not take her *no* as an answer.

He had laughed, believing Mista to be coy. Upon discovering she meant what she said—that she'd rather marry the god Loki—he'd become incensed. Threatening her and her clan was not a way to win her heart.

Aye, Tiernan was definitely a different kettle of Lute fish.

Mista yanked the gown on, and then swiped at some errant hair trailing from the braid she'd hastily fashioned after sword practice with Baldr. There again was another individual who was not happy, but unlike his wife, who just shook her head when in Mista's presence, he'd tried to talk to her about Tiernan: a conversation that had gotten neither of them anywhere.

The tables were being laid for the evening meal when she arrived downstairs. Near the fireplace, Tiernan stood—for once without his usual guards. Perhaps Baldr felt he was no longer a threat.

She slowed her pace and strived for a chieftain like manner.

"Tiernan."

For a moment he stood motionless, the flames highlighting high cheekbones, an expertly sculpted nose, and the one eye she could see of his profile glinted a deep turquoise. Finally he turned.

"Mista." His use of her first name caused her insides to tumble together like a storm-tossed ship.

"'Twould be more respectful to address me as mistress or chieftain." Her admonishment was but a whisper.

"Perhaps, but calling you by your first name is better than the connotations of 'mistress.'" He gave her a look that reeked wicked humor. "I can only imagine what you would be like in bed."

Before she could reply, he continued. "And the word 'chieftain' puts me in mind of someone of Baldr's stature, and you definitely do not match that description." His smile was a slash of white.

"Well...I..." Mista, not usually at a loss for words, stood there for a moment, frozen with the image of sharing a bed with Tiernan. Her cheeks heated with more than the flames of the physical fire.

"I was told you wanted to talk to me. I hope it is to continue our conversation of this morning." His expression grew somber.

"Aye, 'twould be best to handle your outrageous tale and be done with it." She knew she sounded snippy but standing this close to the man did nothing but make her wish for something she couldn't have. He was a thrall, and he was also a bit touched in the head.

"All right. This could take a few moments. Why not be a bit more comfortable?" Tiernan motioned to a small stool near the fireplace.

Mista grasped the material of her gown and then sat down.

"Please tell me your tale from the beginning." She watched as he took a seat on the rushes beside the stool. Perhaps she should chastise him for being so disrespectful as to sit without permission, and from the looks some of her warriors were sending their way, she knew she would hear about this before the end of the evening. Yet, his action only made her want to know what reason he had for acting as her equal.

"Mista, as I told you this morning, I am not from here. I am not even from this country or the boundaries of the world as you would know it. I am from a kingdom made of magical beings." Tiernan batted down the urge to take the hand she clenched in the folds of her gown.

"My world is one of light; no evil is allowed, and no battles have been fought in the last several millennia."

"Millennia? What is this word?" Her question spoke of curiosity and interest, whereas he'd been waiting for the disbelief she'd given him earlier.

He smiled. "One millennium is a thousand years, a span of living and loving. So these mortal battles are not something I'm fond of, especially when I find myself in the midst of clashing swords and battle axes."

For just a fraction of a second, Mista smiled, before her sensual features regained their previously disturbed look.

"How can this be possible?" Her lips pursed into an oval. "If what you say is true, then this place..."

"It's called the Seelie Court, where fae people live." Tiernan supplied the information.

"So, if these people are real, and you are one of them, then that would make you a god." Her blue eyes widened in what could only be dismay and possibly horror.

"No, we are not gods, but we are one of the first creations ever made."

"So what can you do?" Her question was one he'd

been expecting, but hoped she wouldn't ask.

"Normally, I can do all sorts of magick, but because of something I did, I've been banished to your century and cannot use my skills."

Her eyes opened even wider. "Why? What did you do, and what do you mean by my century?"

His sigh was ragged as he tried to find the words to explain the circumstances leading up to his punishment. "To understand what I did, I must tell you a bit of why I did it. My eldest daughter married a mortal, which is strictly taboo. Not only did she break that law but she brought him to the Seelie Court—another infraction of our rules."

Tiernan paused for a moment and looked around. Her warriors, especially Baldr, were giving them the evil eye, as Mista would call it, and he needed to finish his explanations before they broke up the conversation.

"Her husband, though not at that time, was injured mortally. He would have died if she had not brought him to our healer. The other council members were not pleased, and planned on punishing my daughter. I asked to take the punishment myself."

"How noble." Mista too had noticed her men looking their way, but Tiernan's story had drawn her in, but not to the point she believed all he said. Some of his statements waxed of fairy tales told to children.

"Not noble, no, but something most parents would do for their children." His handsome face tinged a bit red at her words.

Hmm...a warrior who blushed. How interesting.

"Please continue." She wanted to get to the heart of his story before Baldr decided to butt into their talk.

"Well, I was sent from the year 2013 and—"

"Impossible. What you speak of is witchcraft." Mista leaned forward. "Do you wish to be burned as a warlock?"

His brows drew together in a frown, and his blue eyes glowed with a silver fire. "I am and will never be a warlock. I am Fae."

For some reason her words had upset Tiernan. The man's attitude became more confusing to Mista. Out of the corner of her eye, she spied Baldr walking their way.

"'Twould be foolish of you to speak of these things you have told me to anyone else."

"Do you believe me, Mista?" His words were low, and the rough timbre of his tone sent a pleasure beat to her heart and the place between her thighs. Her cheeks heated at the thought of this man touching her anywhere he chose.

"I do not know what to believe at the moment, but we will speak again after the evening meal."

"On your feet. 'Tis time for you to go back to your cell." Baldr positively gloated as he reached down to grab Tiernan's arm.

Tiernan jerked his arm away. "I am not a mindless creature to be led. I can stand up on my own." He snarled the words.

"Why you miserable—"

"Stop it, both of you." Mista leveled a glare at Baldr as well as one at Tiernan. For the life of him, the woman in a snit was just as alluring as when she smiled.

"Tiernan is now a thrall, he will be fed and housed with the other thralls." Her words were clipped and even though she continued to stare at him, he felt as if she was seeing something else.

"Baldr, once he has finished supping, I want to talk to Tiernan again." When Baldr opened his mouth in what surely would be an explosive protest, Mista raised her hand, and the overgrown giant's lips smashed together in a grimace.

"Now, if there is nothing else, I am ready to eat." Mista turned and the sensual sway of her hips, although he was sure she would hate to know she caused that type of display, enticed his gaze.

"Stop gawking at Mista unless you want to have your eyes plucked out." Baldr's ears were as red as his face.

"Very well. For the moment, I will keep my stares to myself." Tiernan stood to his feet, and then gave Baldr a mocking bow. "Please lead on."

****

Although the evening meal only lasted an hour or so, Tiernan was more than ready to quit the kitchen when Mista sent for him. He had done nothing but think about whether or not she believed him. And now the fish, mushy vegetables, and oat bread set like a batch of stones in his belly. The warrior escorting him to Mista was not one Tiernan had seen before, and although he didn't try to push him forward, his attitude was one of controlled anger. Baldr had undoubtedly vented his spleen about Tiernan.

He shrugged his shoulders. Nothing to be done about it at the moment but...

The stares of several Vikings pierced him as he moved the last few feet to where their chieftain remained sitting on the dais. He stood and waited for her to acknowledge him.

"I trust you had a good meal, Tiernan." Her words were soft, but although she looked right at him her gaze did not soften. Ah...she displayed her warrior face.

"Yes, thank you." He also kept his tone soft and respectful. It didn't look as if it would take much to stir her men into a berserker frenzy.

Mista stood and then stepped down from the dais. "We will walk outside for a bit of fresh air." When Baldr and her men made to follow their chieftain, she raised her chin just a bit.

"I need no escort, Baldr. Although your diligence to my safety is appreciated, I would not be the Einarsson chieftain if I could not protect myself." With those words, she turned her back on all of them. The lovely sway of her backside caught Tiernan's gaze once more. A sharp shove in the apex of his back almost sent him tumbling into Mista. He sent a murderous glare at the culprit, Baldr, and then waited for her to take the cloak a thrall held, before following the lovely chieftain out the front door.

The night air was chilly, and without his magick to regulate his body temperature, it felt as if he walked into a freezer. He stilled the chattering of his teeth, and then moved to Mista's side. He might have to play the part of a servant in this chapter of his life, but he would not be subservient to a woman he wanted to bed.

Mista turned and Tiernan caught her before she bounced off his body and hit the hard packed earth.

"Oh..." Her exclamation a soft rush of air.

He held her close for a moment, enjoying the thrust of her breasts against his body, his hands caressing the contours of her waist. His shaft filled with blood against her belly, as he felt the softness of her womanhood against the thigh he'd braced to keep her steady. Her feminine but capable hands stroked his chest for one moment, almost shattering his self-control, before she pushed backward away from his touch.

"Thank you. I be not normally so clumsy." Her cheeks, now a pale crimson, showcased the brilliance of her agitated blue gaze.

"Think nothing of it. I'm glad I could help." He withheld the smirk of delight that his close proximity caused her disturbance. Tiernan gently grasped her elbow and tugged her away from the hall. He felt her hesitation but then she squared her shoulders and matched her steps to his.

Once they rounded the stable and were out of view of any warriors prowling the area, he released her. For a moment she stared at him, before directing her gaze to the back door of the building where they housed their horses.

"So do you have any proof that what you say is true?" Mista's question stunned Tiernan. Yes, he had proof, but he couldn't provide it without using his magick. It wasn't that he was that leery of losing his manhood, surely he'd be able to get it back once he returned to the Seelie Court, but for some reason he wanted this woman to believe him without any proof.

He walked a few paces away before returning to her side. "I have no visible proof."

Mista's brows creased in a frown. "Because of your punishment?"

"Yes. I can only ask you to accept my word. A word I have not broken since I came into being."

Chapter Six

Mista could not deny the honesty in Tiernan's gaze. She recognized it as the same look her da had worn on a daily basis until he died.

Still...

She turned and then walked a few feet away. To believe him meant she had to believe all he'd told her. Was it possible? And why did she want to think it so?

"Mista?" His touch on her shoulder, although light, seeped through the layers of clothing to scorch her skin. She spun around, anxious to make it stop. She needed to think, not just about his fantastic tale, but clan business.

"Please... I need to think about what you have told me. 'Tis a lot to take in, and I need—"

"All right. I just need you to answer one thing." Tiernan turned her to face him. As she looked up and caught his gaze, every fiber of her being wanted to believe this man.

"What is it you need?"

"For you to tell me you believe I would not lie to you." His words were soft, his gaze unwavering.

"I want to believe you, but I have to go now." Mista knew it was cowardice pricking her to run, but she did not care. He was too close, too sensual, too much of everything, and she needed to distance herself.

She pulled free from his grasp and began to walk

back to the hall. Halfway there she met Baldr. "Show Tiernan where to sleep, Baldr, and then assign him duties for the morning. I am for bed."

Mista brushed by her second-in-command without another word and once inside she hastened to her bedchamber. After stripping off her clothes she pulled on her bed-gown, banked the fire in the hearth, and crawled into bed.

An hour later sleep still eluded her. What was she going to do about Tiernan? If she actually believed him, and let him go, her clansmen would think she was a weak leader, a female who allowed her softer instincts to sway her. She could not afford that. And why should she? After all, he could not prove any of what he said, so maybe he was one of Erik's men, a traitor sent there to spy on her. Or could he be a chieftain from a clan she didn't know. Sent to possibly arrange an alliance between the clans with her as the prize?

Mista sat straight up in bed. How could she have been so ignorant of all she'd learned? Other than being a bit bloodied when they found him, Tiernan's clothing was in good shape, although unsuitable for their weather. The fact the chain mail he wore did not fit him, something that had bothered her all along, which should have bothered Baldr if he'd not been so set in his mind also weighed into the problem. It had been too big on him, and then last night at dinner and again today when she had placed the collar around his throat, she'd seen the armbands. They were not the apparel of a common warrior. They signified a more royal personage. Either he was an unknown chieftain or...

Her groan competed with the snapping of the fire. All she had done was make her problem worse. And all without touching on the trouble Erik Runolfsson brought to her clan.

Da, how I miss your wisdom.

And in that moment she realized her first responsibility lay with her clan. Come sunrise she would send one of her warriors to infiltrate Erik's holding, to find out if Tiernan was part of a ploy to spy on her by the Runolfsson chieftain. And while she waited on that answer, she would do all she could to find out if he was there by accident or design.

She would not allow his handsome face or pulse-stopping smile to sway her from what was right for her people.

Mista pounded her pillow and then slammed her head back down. Time she got some sleep.

****

Tiernan huddled within the ragged blanket Baldr threw at him after they both returned to the hall. He'd found an empty spot against the wall, and claimed it for his own after issuing a growl at the two canines who'd already bedded down.

The fire had been banked for the night, and the air inside was almost as frigid as outside. If he didn't get out of this situation soon, he'd probably have a good case of frostbite.

The more he thought about it, the more he wanted to use his magick. Surely the council—once they learned of Willamina's machinations—would pardon him for all his crimes.

Yet, how could he be sure, and did he truly want to leave without exploring the uncertain emotions he felt for Mista?

He was sure she was on the verge of believing him,

but then she went distant, afraid, but of what? The only thing he'd done differently was to touch her. Could his touch be abhorrent to her? Or had she felt the same quick ripple of electricity that struck him?

Tiernan closed his eyes and wished again for a chance to change matters. If only he'd challenged Willamina more, fought for the Orb with more than words? Would he be in this situation? And if not, would he forever wonder if perhaps there was a second soul mate for him somewhere in the universe?

****

Willamina strutted up and down the golden throne room, giddy with glee. She'd done it! Tiernan was gone, and the rest of the council was none the wiser as to his destination. When Alex and the others had cornered her about the judgment, she'd fabricated a tale that, if she must say so herself, was brilliant.

"What do you mean, the sentencing is over with?" Alex almost yelled the question at her. At one time she would have thought the dark-haired green-eyed fae to be handsome, but not since he'd gotten married. He'd become stogy and quite unlikable.

"As I told you all"—her gaze encompassed Gideon, a tall silver-haired fae, as well as Jared, chestnut-haired, hazel eyes, and not much on humor— "the sentencing took place after you three failed to show up."

Alex shook his head, his eyes still heavy with his magick-induced nap. "Something is not right, Willamina, and I will be dealing with you." He took a step toward her, but she held her ground. "Now, how did you get the orb out of the cabinet and then put it back without my knowledge?"

Willamina stifled a curse. She'd not expected him to ask that question. And she should have already had an answer. She narrowed her eyes, and then opened her mouth.

"The Orb wasn't necessary. Our dear Tiernan, decided to administer his own punishment." She gauged the reactions on her fellow council members' faces. They were not quite buying it so she needed something believable to seal the deal or else.

"Of course, I don't think the next year with his daughter in the mortal realm is much of a punishment."

"Tiernan is with Catriona?" Jared boomed out the question, but the previous angst in his gaze looked like it faded to relief.

Good. Now to get the other two in a good humor.

"Well, yes, maybe he's hoping she will present him with a grandchild, although I can't imagine why." The shudder that shook her body was not all fabricated.

"I still don't understand why you did not call us to see why we were not here." Gideon's question met with nods from Alex and Jared.

Another question she'd not anticipated.

"I would have, but as I told you, Tiernan decided to deliver his own punishment. A bit presumptuous, but even if I had called you two minutes after the appointed time, you would have missed him."

Willamina smiled, took a deep breath, and hoped the expanse of breast not hidden by her low-cut gown would take their attention away from this damn meeting.

The ploy worked, but not as she would have liked. All three fae wore similar expressions of distaste. No, she hadn't read their minds, although she could, and for a very good reason. She'd encountered the same look from the high-and-mighty trio before. Just as well, it was time for them to go anyway.

"So if there's nothing else, then have an enchanted evening." She crossed the floor and then sat within the spacious refines of the throne.

"Willamina, what do you think you are doing?" Alex roared the question and stalked to where she sat— followed by the other fae.

"I'm getting accustomed to the feel of being a queen." She reveled in their looks of disbelief.

"You cannot be serious. No way did Tiernan appoint you as Queen advocate while he is gone." Gideon's accusatory yell made Alex and Jared's previous ones sound like whispers.

"Well, I'm sorry if you don't believe me. And since there is no way to ask Tiernan without you going into the mortal realm, then I guess you will have to take my word for it." Willamina cut off the giggle trying to escape—the trio looked as if they'd swallowed their wings.

"This is not over, Willamina," Alex warned as he turned to go. "You still have to comply with the council. And believe me, it will not be easy." He paused for the other two fae to catch up and they all left in a blur of misted colors.

"Well, that worked out pretty well." Her words sounded like a gong being pounded in the quiet of the room. She just hoped her plans continued to work out. And to ensure they did, she needed to execute a plan to enchant the council members. And for that she would need the Judgment Orb again. No need in pitting her magick against those three. She'd rather save all her fun for being Queen. Good thing she made a copy of the Orb and put the fake one back in place of the real one.

Chapter Seven

Tiernan's quiet contemplation of the night before had long disappeared by midday. He'd been up since before dawn, mucking out stalls, and now with the evening meal long past, he'd been ordered to replace the food-riddled rushes with new ones.

His steps were tired as he took his armful out back of the kitchen and tossed them onto an already high stack. How long would he have to endure being a slave? And how did those who serve Mista's household stand the knowledge they could never be their own men or women? At least, not unless Mista set them free or they somehow acquired enough coin to buy their own freedom.

"You there, take these and put them down in the hall." A burly house karl, a step above a thrall, thrust clean rushes into Tiernan's arms, and slapped him on the back. If only…

Tiernan threw off what he would do if he used his magick. He'd not yet decided if he would go against his sentence. The consequences of that action would bear more reflection. In the meantime he glared at the karl and received a cuff upside the head for his trouble.

Skull aching, he arrived back inside in time to see Mista striding across the hall. Dressed again as a man in tight leggings and a loose tunic, he wondered if she thought the clothes hid her feminine qualities. Despite his chaotic day, Tiernan smiled. If she did think so, far be it from him to tell her the truth. He was enjoying the view too much.

Mindful of getting hit again, he began to place the rushes in their designated spots, but his gaze kept drifting back to the woman of his thoughts.

"Baldr, I would like to see you in my sitting room, and please bring Olav with you." Mista's words were clipped. Her eyes, when she glanced around the hall and spotted him, turned into blue ice. What the Fae was wrong with her?

Tiernan continued to stare back at Mista until she looked away. Her shoulders shifted backward a bit, and before his eyes she turned into a warrior. Her countenance was as hard as her gaze.

No matter how much he thought about it, he could not come up with a reason her behavior would change from being pensive the prior evening to being cold as the collar around his neck.

A second later, she mounted the stairs leading to the living quarters, and Tiernan placed the last bunch of rushes on the floor. His Fae radar shot sparks at her behavior. And for some reason he just knew his name would be coming up in their meeting.

****

Mista paced the room as she waited on Baldr and Olav to join her. She purposely pushed all thoughts of Tiernan's confused and possibly hurt gaze out of her mind. She needed to concentrate on what was important. And that was her people—nothing else. No one, and that meant the heartbreakingly handsome warrior, would be allowed to interfere with the safety of the clan.

"Mistress?" Baldr's query startled Mista, but she forced herself not to jump like a skittish mare. "Please come in, Baldr, you too, Olav. She motioned to the low bench near her chair. "Please sit."

Once her men did as she requested, Mista got right to the point. "Olav, I want you to go to Clan Runolfsson." She kept her gaze on both men, and when Baldr did not open his mouth, she spoke again.

"Try to blend in with their clan." Mista clenched her fists together. "Aye, I know it could be dangerous, but I need to know if our latest prisoner is one of Erik's friends, since he doesn't quite fit the role of a warrior."

Laughter rolled from Baldr's lips, and while 'twas welcomed, after a few moments of chuckles with Olav joining in, she decided to end their amusement.

"Please, I am not finished." She gave both warriors a look her da had taught her—one that always gained results.

"Pardon, mistress." Baldr's words were a bit choked, and a twinkle danced in his gaze, but Olav looked as serious as a Christian priest speaking of the fires of Hell.

"Now I say this because his demeanor is slightly above a warrior."

At her words, Baldr's mouth flew open.

"Nay, if you would look at him in a different light, Baldr, you would see the truth of my words."

Mista gave him no time to speak as she turned to Olav. "I want you to go in the guise of a blacksmith. You know the trade, you've helped Sigrid, and so you would be believable. Stay at least a sennight, but no more than a fortnight. If you are unable to find out anything by then, there is probably nothing to find out.

At her nod, Olav stood to his feet. "Yes, Chieftain. I will leave before sunrise."

"Thank you, Olav." Mista struggled with duty and like for the young man. "Any time you fear your life is in danger, hie yourself back as quickly as you can. The information is not as important as losing an esteemed warrior."

The young man's shoulders went back even farther, his carriage that of a warrior with twice his experience.

"As you wish."

Mista nodded again, and Olav strode from the room. Baldr remained seated and now she turned to him.

"Baldr, you have given me wise council over the years, even before Da was killed." She moved to seat herself next to her second-in-command. After catching his large hand in hers, she patted his calloused palm. "For that I am grateful. I could not have taken on the role of chieftain without your guidance."

Mista looked into the spears of fire glowing in the hearth. "I also know that without you as my second-in-command my leadership would have been challenged not only by other clans but our own people as well."

"Mista, you owe me no thanks. Your da believed in your ability to rule after him. So did I." Baldr squeezed their connected hands. "*Minn hjarta dóttir*, you have proven yourself to be a respected chieftain."

Baldr's usage of the phrase *my heart daughter* brought tears to her eyes. He'd stepped in even more to guide her in all things in the past years. Yet, his ferocity in protecting her sometimes blinded him to the truth.

She withdrew her hand and then stood to her feet,

moving closer to the hearth. "Thank you, but if 'tis true, then why do you doubt my assessment of Tiernan?"

"Why? 'Tis simple." Baldr's tone sounded strained, and Mista turned back to face him.

"Then please explain it to me. In all other matters you have been my mainstay, the bulwark that shores me up." As she watched, he scraped a hand across his eyes.

"I fear you are allowing tender emotions to interfere with your judgment." He lowered his hand, and she spotted a gleam of silver in his gaze. Something indeed bothered Baldr pertaining to Tiernan, but she could not allow him to think she was a weak woman to be swayed by a pretty face.

"Explain your reasoning." Her tone was harsh.

"What I mean is you are behaving more like a female than a chieftain." Baldr's words were softer than Mista's but nevertheless hurtful in content.

"Baldr, I cannot believe you would think I could be that weak." *Hel!* His words cut Mista like a battle-ax. Never before had he accused her of behaving as a woman.

"Mista, 'tis not what I think. Yet, I have seen you look at this man in a way you have never looked at one of the warriors wanting to court you or even any of our own men."

Her heart fluttered then almost stopped before picking up speed once more. How could Baldr surmise she thought of Tiernan as anything but a prisoner? As she pondered that question scenes from the first time she had glimpsed the man flittered through her head. She *had* treated him differently. Oh, by all that the Christian God claimed holy, how could she have been such a weak-kneed woman?

She would have to handle this as she meant to go on—even if it was to the man she loved as a father.

"So, what if I did? Tiernan is different than past prisoners. You know this. Admit it, Baldr."

"Aye, he does maintain his dignity even when he is poked with ridicule. Not something I would expect from just any man. But Mista, even if he is something other than a warrior, the man is not Viking. He does not belong here, and you wouldst do best to remember that." His words were callous but his gaze held sympathy.

"I know this, and that is why I want to find out if he is here on Erik's behalf. If not, then I propose we let him leave."

She expected Baldr to rage at her suggestion.

"'Tis probably for the best, Mista. If you do plan to stay unwed, then the man needs to be far from here."

She shot Baldr a look. Had he guessed how much Tiernan troubled her? And could he know how much she would love to be Tiernan's for just one night? Did anyone else know? The shock she felt must have shown on her face.

"Rest easy, Mista. No one, not even Gunhilde, has guessed this man is something to you other than me."

The air escaped from her lungs, and she slumped down next to Baldr, her cheek resting against his leather jerkin. "Baldr, what can I do?" Her whisper elicited a pat on the top of her head before he swatted her arm.

"You can do what your da would want. Do what is best for the clan and then you can decide to keep the man or not."

A vibration beneath her cheek caused Mista to raise her head. Baldr's chuckle grew louder and then became contagious.

Once she caught her breath, she patted his chest. "Will I have your blessing if I decide to keep him?"

"Aye, but only after we find out more about him." Baldr's gaze turned serious. "If he is in league with Erik, then you know what will have to be done."

Mista sat up straight. "Aye, I know. And if he is guilty of being an emissary of Clan Runolfsson, I will kill Tiernan myself."

****

Tiernan hammered a nail into the barn wall with enough force the wood splintered. A defect that would warrant him a scolding, yet the repetition of slamming things into inanimate objects soothed him. Why he'd been given what some could call a weapon he didn't know or care. It was a great way to beat down the frustration, anger, and lust, not to mention worry over not seeing Mista at all since she'd gone upstairs the previous day. He'd spent all his evening meal waiting on a glimpse of the petite chieftain only to be disappointed and to end up eating cold food.

After spending a restless night, he'd risen early, and walked outside. He'd watched as one lone Viking rode out before dawn. The man traveled fast and with an odd assortment of tools draped over his saddle. He also looked like the same warrior who'd stood with Baldr in the great hall before Mista placed the slave collar around Tiernan's neck. Why would a Viking only carry a short sword, whereas the rest of his trappings were that of a blacksmith? Tiernan couldn't help but wonder where the man was going.

"Hurry up you. 'Tis time for the morning meal, and past time for you to get to the rest of your chores." The cook, a burly woman who stood almost as tall as Tiernan's six-foot-six frame, waved a ladle at him. He had no doubt she would use it if he didn't make haste. Pity he couldn't just take it away from her and put the fear of the fae inside the woman.

Tiernan shrugged his shoulders, gave the cook a smile that had her fumbling the metal weapon, and then headed for the barn. He needed to see Mista, talk to her, and convince her to release him. But most of all, he wanted her assurance she believed him. Undoubtedly, he'd frightened her with his talk of time travel and the Seelie Court. He picked up a pitchfork and began to shovel hay for the horses. Hopefully, sometime today he would be able to corner the elusive woman and find out where he stood in reference to his freedom and Mista.

The *Thing* judging would be upon him before he knew it, and there was no way in fae he was going to stay a slave or die because of something Willamina had contrived.

Dung hit the wheelbarrow as he started cleaning out the stalls. He needed to hold on and not give in to despair. His fellow fae on the council would sooner or later figure out what the witch had done. Or he hoped.

No, he needed to free himself and then get as far away from Mista and her band of Vikings as possible. Now if he could just get Mista alone.

The day dragged on, and his temper grew hot. He'd missed the midday meal when he'd been ordered to carry firewood into the kitchen. His plan to grab an oatcake or two failed dismally when the cook rapped him on the knuckles with that infernal ladle, and then he'd been shanghaied to brush the horses. The chore in itself should have been soothing but not when every moment he spent doing chores kept him from trying to find Mista.

"You there, take a bucket of water to the practice field and then return to finish your chores." The stablemaster pointed to a wooden bucket.

Tiernan rubbed a hand down the flank of the chestnut before replacing the brush and grabbing the water utensil. The air was crisp, but the sun a welcome change from a cold mist that had fallen the day before. As he neared where the warriors practiced he heard the clang of swords and the occasional profanity and laughter that echoed around the area set aside for practice.

He sat the bucket on the ground near where the warriors battled and watched the warfare. A Viking about the size of Baldr was engaged in battle-ax play with the spur in Tiernan's ass. The feint to the right earned Mista's second-in-command a mock jab from his sparring partner.

Tiernan's gaze lit on each pair of warriors as they sliced and diced with their weapons. The scene before him paled without the fire-swords of his homeland. Although what he'd told Mista was correct, they had no war in his world, it didn't mean that male fae did not practice their skills during a twice-weekly battle-royal. All vied to have a chance to challenge him in a brief battle.

Perhaps he would up the amount of time spent in war practice when he returned home—whenever that may be.

As he watched the main body of warriors branched out and then formed a semi-circle around two particular combatants. The taller of the two was built like a mountain, and his dark hair fanned out as he dodged the blows from the smaller warrior. As they moved in a circle, Tiernan's gaze followed the movements of both Vikings. Whereas the first warrior's hair was loose, the other had tied his hair back in a long braid—a braid that glowed reddish-blonde in the weak sun. His gaze locked on the leather cupping a backside that was feminine and sensual in design.

Mista!

Chapter Eight

His heart took a dive toward his feet as Mista moved in closer to the giant she was fighting. Her blows were hard and at times found substance against the physique of the other. But then her opponent would also strike home. Although they used only the flats of their swords and no blood trickled down to pool on the hard ground, Tiernan still wanted to snatch Mista away from the warrior. The man's gaze seemed overly familiar when he gazed on his chieftain. Who was he? Why had he not seen him before? And what was he to Mista?

Baldr broke away from the duel and strode to where Tiernan stood. He cupped his hands in the cold water, splashed some on his face, and then took a few sips of a fresh handful. Once finished he eyeballed Tiernan as a snake would a mouse.

"So what do you think of our fighting sport?" The man's words were casual, almost friendly in tone, and sent a blade of distrust straight to Tiernan's spine.

"I think that men should find a better way to settle their differences than to fight." He meant his statement to be inflammatory, but Baldr laughed.

"I suspect you believe in a lot of things, and you would do your best to persuade Mista to believe you."

Still no sign of displeasure in the man's tone.

The blade dug deeper.

"And what if I do convince her?" He watched Baldr for any movement that would signal the prequel to cleaving Tiernan in half.

"Then you best make sure that you do not lie to her." The Viking brought the battle ax around and lightly stroked the blade. "Mista is like my own daughter. I would not only maim someone who hurt her but also suffer them to die a painfully slow death."

Their gazes collided and Tiernan did not look away. "That's good. I would feel the same way if someone hurt her."

"Why? You do not know her well enough to care."

"And in your eyes no one could. Trust me. I have lived long enough to know that caring for another can come softly like a warrior creeping through the night, or it can fall on you like a horse in battle."

"Your words are true, but your situation in life is that of a slave." Baldr's words were not cruel and might have found grace inside Tiernan's mind if he weren't already torn apart over his feelings for Mista.

"There you are wrong. I am no one's slave. I am here by someone's malicious act of hatred, and I will leave a free man."

"And where will you go if you are judged innocent?" Baldr shot a look toward Mista and her fighting partner.

"Back home when I can. I have responsibilities to my people, my family, and a judgment of my own to hold." He too glanced at Mista. Her breath came in little spurts of misted air, her breasts rising and falling under the linen tunic she wore with a vest that barely covered the mounds of flesh.

"And what of Mista? How would she figure in your

plans?" The question hit Tiernan like the aforementioned horse. Could he take her away from her clan, would she consider leaving?

"That would be up to her." He clenched his fists as he watched the dark warrior smile down at Mista. Something about the man grated on his nerves. He had no right to drape an arm around his chieftain's shoulder.

"So who is this Viking handling your chieftain in such a familiar manner?" His question shot into the air just as all of those in the fighting area fell silent.

Mista's head turned toward Tiernan, as did all the warriors. Her blue gaze held surprise as well as shock. She stayed motionless as her sparring partner moved to stand within a foot of Tiernan.

"'Twould be best for you to keep your mouth shut, slave." He growled the words.

"And *'twould* be best if you did not manhandle Mista." He knew his words would be like waving a plump bird in front of a starving man, but he didn't care. Tiernan was fed up.

"Why, you maggot, you are nothing more than a flea in my dog's ass."

"And if I were your dog, I'd run away from a man who has such poor manners." Tiernan caught the look of disbelief on Baldr's face, and then the man gave a slight smile. Would wonders never cease?

"I could have you killed for your insolence."

Tired of fencing verbally, Tiernan decided enough was more than plenty. "So it seems you are too cowardly to fight me in a fair fight—one on one."

A gulp of air exploded from Baldr, cries of what could only be encouragement to kill Tiernan erupted from the warriors, but from Mista there was nothing.

The Viking he baited growled.

"So do you want to fight or stand around and grouse like an old woman?" Tiernan's continued badgering caused the man's brown eyes to widen, and one meaty fist closed in a slight thud.

"To the death?"

"Let's just say that whomever draws the first blood wins. I would not want to upset Mista."

"Tiernan, no." Mista made her way to him through the men gathering around. They reminded him of wild creatures who smelled blood. Her sorrowful gaze evoked both warmth and anger. He knew she thought he would get himself killed, he also knew she would believe it was her fault.

"Mista, do not trouble yourself over this wormy slave. He will die and then—"

Her eyes flashed in what looked like a glimpse of anger. "Nay, Magnor. You will only fight for first blood. Anything more and you will answer to me. Is that clear?"

Tiernan could have shouted with glee. There was the chieftain he knew and was beginning to love. Her voice was strong, her countenance brooking no argument as she faced up to Magnor.

Magnor on the other hand looked like someone had stomped on his sword hand. "You forget I am not one of your warriors, but a friend of longstanding to your family. Would you sever the relationship between your clan and the clan of Bjornasson?

"Nay, but I will not suffer an attitude that is nothing more than male nonsense." Mista turned her gaze to Tiernan. "You should not have spoken to Magnor at all being a slave."

Her words not only wounded Tiernan but the fact she must think him as nothing but dirt beneath her boots, enraged him as well.

"You forget, but allow me to remind you, Chieftain Einarsson. I am not a slave. I am a king in my homeland. You would do best to remember this, for retribution can come in many ways."

Mista gasped at Tiernan's tone and words. The man actually cared nothing for his well-being. She could have him put down for speaking to her as he did. Yet her heart would not allow it. She should have couched her admonishment better. Now all she'd done was add more wood to the fire of male arrogance.

"Silence, or I will cut the tongue out of your insolent mouth." Baldr's blade was at Tiernan's throat, but he did not show any fear. Why? Had his banishment to a strange land and time damaged his mind? No one who suffered Baldr's rage did so without quaking in terror.

"Then I suggest you try, old man." Tiernan's arm shot up in a movement so swift that Mista barely saw him grasp Baldr's wrist. A slight press of his fingers above Baldr's leather glove, and his weapon fell to the ground with an eerie clatter. Baldr grabbed his arm and glared at Tiernan.

"What kind of magick did you use to send electricity into my arm?"

His shouted question caused the other warriors to back away. Magick of any kind was considered evil by her clan.

"No magick, just something I learned from fighting with my own *warriors*."

Baldr's lips relaxed from a grimace into a circle of

69

disbelief if Mista wasn't mistaken.

"So, Magnor, do we fight or not?" Tiernan stood motionless as did Mista waiting for Magnor's answer.

"Aye, you whelp of a jackal." Magnor's gaze wasn't as certain as before, and she wondered if he was having second thoughts. She prayed he would change his mind.

Tiernan reached down, deftly grabbed Baldr's abandoned weapon, and then gave a slight bow to his opponent. "I am ready when you are."

Both men moved as one into the circle previously filled with warriors. Warriors who now branched out until they looked like a wall of Vikings surrounding the pair. Mista pushed through the crowd of men to stand by Baldr, whose gaze held an anticipation she usually only glimpse on the battlefield. Wagers were being shouted out on whom her men thought would win. The odds lay with Magnor.

"So, Baldr, why are you not betting?"

"Only a few moments ago I would have bet my entire weaponry and my horse on Magnor, but now... I be not so sure on the outcome of this fight." He sounded confused, but not altogether displeased.

"You do not seem to be upset at the thought that Tiernan might actually win." She placed her hand on his arm, and he looked down at her.

"Nay, I think 'twould be a good thing to have your man beat Magnor."

"Why?" She wanted to also ask why he thought Tiernan was hers, but instead clenched the sleeve beneath her grip with trembling fingers as Tiernan and Magnor circled one another.

"Let us just say that this warrior you would have

me give a chance, just might not be the weakling I thought he was."

Before she could voice her surprise, Magnor's sword slashed deadly under the now low hanging clouds. The downward motion would have cleaved Tiernan in half if it had found its mark. He jumped back and then brought his own weapon up to tangle with Magnor's. The ringing of blades shattered the calls for wagers, and with a one arm thrust, Tiernan sent Magnor reeling back a step. Anger glowed bright in the Viking's gaze as he shifted forward on his right foot to swing once more at Tiernan. Again, Tiernan sidestepped, and brought his own weapon to bear, this time to rest against the leather shirt Magnor wore.

Mista held her breath as she waited to see if Tiernan would indeed draw first blood. When he only laughed her heart clenched with fear. He was baiting Magnor. A fool-hardy stunt that could get him killed.

"Well, well, the pretty-boy is more of a warrior than either of us gave him credit for." Baldr grinned at Mista, but she wanted nothing to do with his amusement. She remained silent, and the battle continued as Tiernan gave another slight bow.

Magnor's growl plummeted the blood in her veins to a freezing level. She needed to stop them before someone was killed. Deep in her heart she knew the Viking would not allow Tiernan to live, not if he wanted to keep his pride intact.

The heavier warrior stepped back, brought his blade up in an arc, and then proceeded to swing with all his might at Tiernan's head. Her gasp was played back several times by all whom watched. Baldr's expression went from concentrated interest to horrified. If the blow found flesh and bone, Tiernan would be dead, and Magnor would be violating a direct order—as well as abusing a chieftain who offered him hospitality.

Mista moved forward, intent on stopping the two men, but Baldr caught her arm and held her back. "Let me go, Baldr."

"Nay, Mista. Watch pretty boy." She did as he asked, and found herself amazed. Tiernan not only didn't look upset over his almost-decapitation, but he motioned to Magnor to try again. How incredibly ignorant and infantile were men! Again, she darted forward, and again Baldr stalled her efforts.

"Well, Magnor, do you care to admit defeat now?" Tiernan's grin normally would warm Mista's heart, but the smile he wore did not reach his eyes. The wind began to stir and blew colder air into the arena, chilling Mista who waited for Magnor's answer.

"It will be my honor to send you from this life." He raised his sword once more and with an ear-splitting roar rushed Tiernan.

Tiernan's body hit the ground with a thud hard enough to rattle his teeth—not to mention bounce his brain around. He shook it off and jumped to his feet. Thankful his sword had not fallen as well, he gripped it tighter as Magnor regrouped and spun around to face Tiernan once more.

Enough. He might not be able to use his magick, but he would finish this fight—now.

Magnor drew close enough that he could see the berserked look in his gaze, glimpse the spittle dotting his lower lip, and the muscles flexing in his sword arm.

Tiernan held his stance, his body rigid, his inner muscles aching to move, but he waited. When Magnor

was close enough to strike, he still held his ground—
ignoring the gasps of the men around him as well as the
softly uttered, "Nay," from Mista.

He watched the weapon begin its downward spiral
until it was only six inches from his head.

Chapter Nine

Tiernan ducked, slid under Magnor's arm, and then sent the flat of his own sword into the back of the Viking's knees.

Dirt puffed up in little granules when Magnor went down. Tiernan placed his blade against the back of his opponent's neck. The silence following his act was so complete he could almost hear the now-falling snow flutter to the ground.

A quick nick and he replaced the sword with his foot. Pandemonium erupted around him. Baldr pressed through the crowd of Vikings surrounding Tiernan. Some of the men slapped him on the back, before tugging him away from Magnor who warned off those who would help him rise with a heated growl. Mista stood by herself, her petite stature straight and regal, but in the split of a second, he saw her ball her trembling fingers into a fist.

She did care if he lived or died. Tiernan wanted to go to her, but Baldr reached his side. The slap he received from this man made the others feel like one of the snowflakes.

"I guess I will be finding you a new name." Baldr grinned.

"Tiernan will do. I like it better than *Pretty Boy*." He smiled back, but he wanted to talk to Mista.

"I need to talk to Mista." He walked to where she

stood.

"You realize this changes nothing. You will still be a slave until the *Thing* ruling." Her words pelted him like an arrow into the marrow of his bones. Her blue eyes were shadowed, and not just from the wintry weather. He wanted to take her in his arms, but not now, not when he needed answers.

"Why? Was it because I fought Magnor? Or was it because I proved to your warriors I am more than a slave?"

"How can you say that? And you should not be speaking such to me. I am the—"

"Yes, I know what you are. Chieftain to your clan, but can you not be a woman for once?"

Mista gasped and drew her arm back.

"Make no mistake, I will not tolerate another blow from anyone today."

"I wasn't…" Her voice trailed off and she looked at the ground.

Beneath the mantle of chieftain, Mista looked fragile. He hated that he was the cause of her distress, but she must understand what her men already did. Yes, he'd told her he was a king, a free man, but it seemed she was not yet ready to believe or trust him.

"I think it would be best if we talk later. Right now, I am going to go back to the stables." Tiernan walked through the crowd of men, and even shook hands with one or two, but his mind was no longer on his win over Magnor. It was on what else he could do to convince Mista to believe the truth before the *Thing* took place.

****

Mista managed to elude Baldr for most of the afternoon, and Magnor had left for home, right before the evening meal. His parting had not been pleasant. Now it seemed her luck had run out in avoiding more controversy.

"Mista, 'tis no good ignoring me. We need to talk." Baldr's gruff voice came right at her ear as she tried to scoot beneath the stairs. Wishing she could turn into a mouse and just disappear didn't happen so...

"All right. What do we need to talk about?"

"Do not be taking that peevish attitude with me, girl." His words irritated her. She was more than tired of being told what to do, what to say.

She huffed back. "I am your chieftain. I can take any tone or attitude I like."

"Then you will be finding a new second-in-command. Your da would be twisted in death to know you would speak to me this way." Baldr sounded a tinge hurt, which was not what she wanted at all. But then again, she couldn't have what or whom she wanted.

"You be right. I am sorry. It has been more than a trifle upsetting day." Her apology found favor when he chuckled and then joined her by bounding down the half-dozen steps separating them.

"Would you like to go to your sitting room or step outside? The snow isn't deep enough to spoil your house slippers."

The twinkle in his eyes was contagious.

"I think you need to look again, old one. I am still wearing my boots."

"Good, now all you will need is a cloak." Baldr grabbed her arm, spun her around, and led her through the dining area. Once outside he pulled her over to a bench and pushed her gently down on the oak wood.

"So what do you want to talk about, Baldr?" Mista plucked at a loose thread on the cloak.

"About Tiernan." Baldr's gaze didn't have the fiery blaze it normally had when discussing the prisoner.

"What about him?"

"I be not sure you can keep him as a slave. The man has won respect from all of your warriors." He sounded a bit amazed at Tiernan's feat. She wondered if that had been Tiernan's intent all along.

"The law is the law, Baldr. You know that." She looked out toward the practice field, and wondered if Tiernan was still in the stables.

"Aye, I agree, but as much as I hate to admit it, you were right about him being different but wrong about him not being a warrior. The man is skilled in fighting. I know we are waiting on Olav's return, but I think for now, you could allow him to work with the warriors and not do menial labor."

"You truly think the men would accept him? What about his slave collar?" Mista looked Baldr square in the eyes.

"Leave the collar, but allow him to behave as a man. Judge him by his behavior with the men." He patted her shoulder. "If he behaves as he did with Magnor, then I think he will make an excellent addition to our warriors."

Mista stood up and walked away from the bench. The stars above her hung a row of candles dotting the dark night. The snow dressed the ground with a thin cloak of white, and for the moment the world was silent.

Snow drifted down. Mista stuck her hand out and caught a flake on her palm. She brought it to her mouth and tasted the icy treat. Her gaze once again scanned the sky overhead. One star seemed just a bit brighter than the others. She wondered if Tiernan's home rested between the constellation and earth.

She needed to either believe his fantasy story or not. She couldn't keep on feeling like she did. One moment she wanted him as a woman wants a man, the next she was frightened of him being a Fae king as he called it, and she was certain he would leave when he could.

Mista shook her head, and turned back to Baldr.

"You be right. He needs to train with the men. I will make a decision on freeing him once Olav is back." She allowed the hand Baldr placed on her shoulder to remain.

"And if we find out he is innocent for certain?"

"Then I will remove the slave collar and he can leave."

****

Confused did not even cover Tiernan's emotions. On his way to the kitchen to see if the cook had any chores for him he'd been waylaid by Baldr. Their conversation had been more than interesting.

"Tiernan." Baldr clapped a hand on his shoulder, but Tiernan refused to flinch. The old codger had a firm and sometimes punishing touch.

"What can I do for you, Baldr?" He allowed a smile to crease his lips but remained wary. Baldr's congenial attitude of that afternoon had thrown him off his stride, and now the grin on the Viking's face made his fae radar go off.

"Your fight this afternoon was well done. Magnor would have not hesitated in killing you even with the dictate of only first blood. You exhibited Viking courage and a warrior's heart. You could have killed him, but in not doing so you earned my respect as well as the rest of the Einarsson warriors."

"And does this allow me to be released as a slave?" He watched Baldr's eyes. The twin orbs of brown looked everywhere but at Tiernan.

"Not right now…" Baldr turned his gaze to meet Tiernan's. "But you have been promoted to practice with our warriors. You are no longer to work at slave chores."

Not exactly what he was hoping for, but he'd take what he could get. "And when is this supposed to start?"

"Now."

"All right. So do I get a weapon of my own, and will I be able to talk to Mista without hordes of Vikings listening in?"

For a moment, Baldr's pleasant expression changed to stone, but then his massive body relaxed. "Best you convince Mista to speak with you first, and worry about privacy later. Tomorrow, report to the practice field after the morning meal."

Baldr strode off toward the main hall, and Tiernan made a hasty exit outside. He found a bit of privacy in the winter-shrouded garden. A tree barren of leaves served as a backrest, while he sorted through Baldr's announcement.

So with his newly found freedom he needed to find Mista and talk with her. Surely with Baldr in his camp, they could come to a reasonable bargain and Tiernan could be on his way once the slave collar was removed.

****

Tiernan crept up the stairs to Mista's living quarters. His original plan to speak with her after the evening meal had not materialized. His prey had not come down to break her fast, so with a lot of trepidation (just in case his freedom did not extend beyond the first floor and the outside) he planned to breach her chamber.

The thought brought warmth to Tiernan that threatened to have his male part waving like an untried youth. And try as he might he couldn't disassociate the combination of Mista and the chamber she slept in. The hour wasn't all that late, but the petite chieftain rose early, so she might already be in bed.

He eased onto the landing and tried to put all thoughts of what she might or might not be wearing out of his mind. He wasn't even sure which room was hers. Without his magick he'd have to take a chance on opening each door and glancing in.

A click down the hallway startled him, and he braced back against the cold wall. Gunhilde, Baldr's wife, stepped out of a doorway at the end of the corridor. He held his breath waiting to see which direction she would move. There was nowhere for him to go except back down to the lower level. A sigh of relief escaped quietly as she entered a room not far from where he hoped Mista rested.

The second the door closed, Tiernan walked to the room she'd just left. Should he knock? If he did he would probably raise Baldr's wife who from what he'd seen was the equivalent of a fishwife in this time. He lifted the latch and gently pushed the door inward. After stepping over the threshold, he scanned the room. A fire blazed in the hearth, a bathing tub stood devoid of a body, and the bed was empty of the woman he'd come to find.

He eased further into the room. A body hit his, and he lost his balance. He stumbled but did not fall. An arm encircled his throat, and then he felt a sharp prick.

"Who are you? What do you want?" Mista's questions were punctuated with another quick nick of the blade. If she kept on he'd be full of holes.

"It's Tiernan. Now put down the knife so we can talk." In the split moment the blade moved, he reached back and then pulled her body around until she settled in his arms. The blade made no sound when he tossed it onto the bed.

It was then he realized he held a *naked* woman in his arms. By the way Mista's blue eyes widened, she must have reached the same conclusion.

Her fists hit his shoulders like pebbles hitting a tin roof. But for all her femininity, she did pack a punch. Maybe he should try to remember she was not just a beautiful woman, but also the Viking who held his freedom in her hands.

"Mista, I'll put you down if you stop pummeling me." He hid a grin as she withdrew her hands in a quick motion.

"Fine. Then please be putting me down now." Her words were breathless and did nothing to quiet the passion rising to fit snugly against his pants. He should put her down, but on second thought, maybe he would hold her a bit longer.

Chapter Ten

Mista opened her mouth once more to tell Tiernan to put her down, but his lips descended so quickly all she could do was brace herself for the heat his kiss brought. Her arms wrapped around his neck as if they belonged to someone else. She should fight the feelings he invoked inside her, but instead she welcomed the caress of his mouth—a caress with enough heat to melt the newly fallen snow.

Although not experienced in the art of love-making, her instincts prompted her to touch the tip of the tongue he moved gently beyond her lips with her own. The thrust and parry sent another wave of molten fire to her feminine center.

She moaned inside his mouth, and the arms holding her tightened. The kiss continued until Mista feared she would pass out before it ended. Finally Tiernan gently unsealed their lips and then carried her to the bed.

Seated now on his lap, she had no strength to speak, let alone flay him for taking advantage of her. And truthfully she was not sure she wanted to.

Mista raised her gaze to meet his. The blue of his eyes were now deep silver. The metallic gleam intensified when he lowered his head. The caress of his tongue against the arc of her neck caused her limbs to go weak. The hand that had dropped to her waist when they sat down traced a path to her breasts. His fingers tweaked one of her already peaked nipples, and she stifled another moan.

She should not allow him such liberties. She was a chieftain, but now in the dark with only the fire casting a glow to their features, she had a hard time remembering that significant fact.

Tiernan's hand palmed her breast, warm against her water-dotted skin. Fire of a kind she'd never experienced built and settled between her thighs. She resisted the urge to press her legs together.

"Mista…" The sound of her name on his lips bathed her in a different warmth. He sounded so gentle, so loving, so…

She needed to focus on how he'd gotten into her room, and what he wanted. There were still too many facts she needed to know about this man. Even though her heart wanted to put her trust in him completely, she could not—would not—for her clan's sake.

Fighting her body's desire, Mista struggled to get off of his lap, found her robe, and tugged it on.

Tiernan watched as Mista tied the material closed, covering up the seductive curves he'd so enjoyed viewing and touching. He'd allowed her to leave him for one reason. He did not want his attempt to love her to be thrown back in his face as a ploy to take advantage of her nakedness.

No, he'd rather stand down, if his swollen flesh would only do just that.

"Tiernan, I think you should leave." Her blue eyes were misty with what he hoped were the banked embers of desire. Surely she'd felt the same wondrous sensation of drowning as he had.

"In a bit, but for right now we need to talk."

Knowing he would only have a few moments, at the most, to persuade her of his intent, he stood and moved away from the bed.

"Perhaps in the morning would be better." Mista walked to the door. Before she could open it, Tiernan moved to stop her.

"No, now, Mista. Please…" His entreaty found substance when she gave a ragged sigh.

"Very well, but then you must leave. If Baldr finds…"

"I know. He will try to skewer me with his sword." The grin he cast her way met with disbelief.

"Be ye insane? 'Tis not a jesting circumstance." She wrapped her arms around her waist.

"No, it is not, but I do not fear Baldr—only you." Tiernan waited to see what response she would give to his words.

"Why would you fear me?"

"Think of it. You hold my freedom in your hand. Not to mention you have stolen a bit of my heart." The last part he'd planned to keep to himself, but somehow his heart overruled his mind.

"Tiernan, you barely know me. And as for your freedom, that will be decid—"

"You would still subject me to your version of justice? You would humiliate me by having me brought up before men who I am equal to at this *Thing's* judgment?" His fists clenched as he tried to rein in his anger.

"Nay, but there are matters I need to have straight in my mind before I release you or pass sentence." She held up her hand when he would have spoken.

"You will not have to be brought up before our

court, but there is still the matter of why you were on Einarsson lands in the first place."

"I told you how I came to be here." He scrubbed his hand through his hair. Wanting nothing more than to shake the woman and make her see sense. Had nothing he told her found root? Did she truly believe he had lied about his birthright? And his status as a king?

"Yes, I know what you told me, but Tiernan, it still seems a preposterous tale."

Hurt pounded his chest with claws of iron. He'd told her his story, and still she chose not to see the truth.

"Preposterous is trying to make love to a woman who you thought trusted you. I have done none of your people any harm. I have told you all about myself." Tiernan took a few steps away from Mista.

"Tiernan…I…"

"Forget it, Mista. I will go back to the stables and be a good boy. I will practice with your men, and then just maybe I will convince you of what I already know. I am not a liar."

Before she could say anything, he retraced his steps to the door. She stepped back and he raised the latch. A second later he was in the hallway. A few moments more he was on his way to the stables. He could have stayed in the great hall, but tonight he wanted the company of the beasts he'd taken care of, and the solitude to lick his wounds.

****

Mista crawled into bed and failed to stop the tears from soaking her pillow. Beneath the anger and disbelief in Tiernan's eyes she'd witnessed the hurt he held back.

It was not her intent to hurt him, but he had taken

her by surprise appearing in her chamber. She'd come so close to cutting his throat before realizing the identity of her visitor.

She picked up the knife where it rested at the foot of the bed and held it aloft. Tiernan could have died by her hand.

And just how would you feel about that, Mista?

The blade clattered on the night table. If Tiernan had died from her actions she would have been devastated. But what she'd done to him was almost as bad. Why was it so hard for her to believe his tale of Fae, kings, and a magical world?

Because if she believed him, once he regained his freedom he could return home. An event she did not want to think about. His presence in the last week had made her life fuller. Mista buried closer into her pillow. Was she so pitiable she needed a man to make her feel better?

Or could it be that she had finally found a man she could respect? Love even, if circumstances were different. Nay, best to put Tiernan from her mind. He would make a good warrior until Olav returned with hopefully the answers to her questions.

After hitting her pillow more times than necessary she tried to sleep. Yet, dawn with all its beautiful homage made an appearance before Mista managed to fall into a restless doze.

****

Tiernan spent a sleepless night to rise just as the sun began to come up. He had come so close to making love to Mista.

Fae's wings, he wanted her so badly, but if he used his brain instead of his shaft, he knew it would be wrong to take her to bed when he had no plans to stay in her homeland or the ninth century.

He bathed quickly in a bucket of water he drew from one of the wells near the stables. After grabbing a hunk of cheese and a flat of bread, he munched his way through his unsatisfactory breakfast, and then washed it down with a tankard of mead. Baldr and the other warriors were on his heels as he walked to the practice field.

"Hold up, lad." Baldr's greeting sounded friendly enough, but Tiernan couldn't help but wonder if Mista had told him about their previous night's meeting.

He stopped and waited for her second-in-command to catch up. "Good morning, Baldr."

"You be ready to work hard today?" The question caused a chuckle to erupt from Tiernan's throat.

"As opposed to stable work being easy?" His response drew laughter from Baldr, and the warriors close enough to hear it.

"True, you have worked hard, but now you will be pitting yourself against hardened men and not animals and dung." Baldr grinned.

"Yes, and I am more than ready to exercise my sword arm." Tiernan gave a slight bow to Baldr before straightening.

"Then you will be needing a weapon." The older Viking held up one of the two swords he carried.

"You are actually trusting me with a weapon?"

"Aye lad, but use it wisely. If for one moment I think you might use it on one of us in other than practice play, then I will not hesitate to gut you." Although the words were uttered in a pleasant tone, the hard glint in Baldr's eyes showed he spoke the truth.

Tiernan took the sword Baldr offered and then moved to the practice circle. Almost immediately a Viking stepped in front of him.

The man grinned before introducing himself. "I be Simund." Without another word the warrior brought up his weapon and begin to slash the air in front of Tiernan in a mock attack. Stepping back a few steps he raised his blade and waited for the Viking to make another move.

A quick downward thrust from his sparring partner, and Tiernan found himself on the defense. Both blades met and rang out in the early morning air.

As if it were a signal other partners took their places and soon the practice field hosted a force of sweating men, screaming swords, and cries of battle. Tiernan wasn't sure how much time passed, but he'd gone from one partner to four. His tunic was soaked through, and every muscle he had begged for mercy. Finally when he thought his arm would break from the exertion Baldr called a halt.

He walked to the water bucket with careful steps. No need in showing the others he was indeed out of shape. The fight with Magnor had been fueled by jealousy and anger, but he definitely needed to put in some practice time.

After quenching his thirst he moved back out of the way. Only a moment passed before he was joined by Baldr.

"You did well, Tiernan."

"Thank you. It's been a while since I practiced quite so hard."

His words garnered him a slap on the back—hard enough to have him rocking on his heels. After a brief hesitation he joined the laughter spewing from the man at his side.

"Well, you did not show it and that says a lot for your determination. We will practice more after we eat, but first, I have some questions." Baldr's humor seemed to fly off his back as quickly as drops of anxiety jumped forward to plague Tiernan.

If Mista had shared any of their encounters, he could very well die before he had a chance to return home.

But if Baldr knew of their aborted lovemaking wouldn't the man have skewered him on the field?

"All right. I'm at your service." Tiernan deliberately kept all sense of apprehension from his tone.

"Let's walk out a bit." Baldr lifted his arm toward the gates of the courtyard. Tiernan followed holding his sword down by his side. He'd not been given a sheath to house the blade, but he did not want to leave it behind.

The wind began to pick up as they made their way over to ice and snow-coated trees. Baldr leaned back against one of the trunks and Tiernan followed his example. "So, what did you want to ask me?"

"I would like to know about your background. Where do you come from really?" Baldr gave him a hard look, but his expression also contained curiosity.

"You want the story I told to Mista that you and your warriors could not hear?" He regretted the harsh inflection in his tone. Now was not the time to make the Viking angry.

"Yes, the one that has her doubting herself as chieftain." Baldr returned the harsh tone two-fold.

"She does not need to doubt herself. My tale is a bit hard to believe for any time period, let alone this one."

"Time period?" The gaze that caught Tiernan's was interested. At least he wasn't calling for someone to drown or burn him as a warlock. At least not yet.

"Perhaps my tale would be better told over tankards of mead, and somewhere a bit warmer." He hoped his idea would buy him time to decide how much to tell this man. Baldr wasn't just the leader of Mista's warriors, but he cared deeply for the woman.

"Aye, we will speak after the afternoon training."

"Where?"

"In my chamber. My wife will be serving Mista or helping with the evening meal preparations." Baldr straightened up and looked at Tiernan again. "Now we best be grabbing a bite to eat and then back to work."

Chapter Eleven

Mista stayed away from the practice field that morning. She occupied herself during the noon meal by going through the contents of her weapons trunk. And if some misguided soul thought she was hiding from Tiernan, then… she would just have to stab him. Yes, she was avoiding the man like an unwanted sore. He had messed with her mind and her body. And how was she supposed to believe him about anything?

What she did know was she needed to control her emotions. She was a chieftain—the leader of her people. Mista would not hide in her chamber to avoid a warrior. She would go to the practice field to see how *all* her warriors were doing.

Flakes of white once again fell. She could hear the shouts coming from the mock battles, and wondered if—

No. She would not wonder. She was entitled to *know* how Tiernan performed. The word caused heat to bathe her face, warming her from the chilled air. The man knew his way around a bedchamber, and his prowess against Magnor proved he could fight. Yet, Mista knew she needed to distance her female wants from what was best for her clan.

The men were in groups of three instead of two. It only took her a moment to find Tiernan's tall and broad-shouldered frame. Long hair bound in a braid, he once again wore the sleeveless black tunic he'd had on when they first met. The only adornments against his naked and muscular arms were the armbands. Mista needed to ask him about those. She should have already done so.

Did he not feel the cold?

She certainly had not the night before. The blaze in her body had rivaled the heat from the flames in her chamber. She wondered what it would feel like to experience that type of inferno again. To have Tiernan make love to her completely.

The man surely tied her up in knots, and she was uncertain of how to untangle them.

Bedeviled with her thoughts, Mista did not realize the men had taken a break until Tiernan spoke.

"Afternoon, Mista." His voice resembled a low hum of sensuality. How could he make such a simple greeting sound so intimate?

"And a good afternoon to you, Tiernan."

"I missed seeing you at practice this morning and when we broke our fast." His words, couched as a statement, sounded quizzical in nature. She turned away to gaze across the training field.

Mista's eyes had gone from a soft blue to a harder azure before she'd looked away. Something bothered her.

"Baldr normally trains the men. I have complete confidence he instructed you well in how we fight." Her words were clipped as she turned back to face him.

"He did an excellent job, but I missed *you*." He cautiously touched her arm. She yanked away from his touch.

"What's wrong, Mista?

"There be nothing wrong. I have been busy. And besides, I owe you no explanation for anything." She flashed him a look that would have cut him in half if she'd been armed with more than her enticing gaze.

"I beg to differ. I wondered how you would react after last night. Now I know." Tiernan taunted her.

"You know what?"

"That you are afraid to feel like a woman. For too long you have been trying to be a man, the chieftain of your clan." He watched with interest as Mista clenched her fists, and her cheeks took on a pink hue that had nothing to do with the chilly afternoon.

"You know nothing about me. Nothing." She raised her hand, but instead of allowing her to slap him as he knew she wanted to he caught the flimsy weapon and kissed her palm.

"You go too far, slave." Her words were like a slap in the face for Tiernan.

"No, I have not gone far enough." He grabbed her arm and pulled her close. The smell of roses, the startled look in her eyes, and his rising need to conquer her as she needed to be conquered overrode his common sense. His head lowered, his lips a scant inch from hers when he heard a noisy "Ahem."

Still holding her hand, he turned and found Baldr standing almost hip-to-hip at his side. "Go away." Tiernan growled.

"Nay, lad, 'tis best if you come with me and we have that bit of a talk." Baldr caught his arm, and squeezed just hard enough to cause Tiernan to release Mista's hand. The Viking then tugged him away from the field and into the castle.

After almost being dragged up the stairs, all

without any additional conversation from Baldr, Tiernan's banked temper began to spike. Once in a chamber not quite the size of Mista's his arm was released.

"Have a seat." Baldr motioned toward a bench near the window. Tiernan did as he asked, but was none too happy to oblige. The pane of glass, which if history was correct was not commonplace in Viking time, had misted from the combination of the fire in the hearth, and the cold air outside.

"Look, boy…" Baldr's words trailed off when Tiernan shot him a glance of disbelief. Of course the man could not know he was thousands of years his senior, but still…

"Tiernan, I know that you have feelings for Mista. 'Tis been clear almost since the moment you arrived."

Tiernan jerked his gaze to Baldr's. Was it true, had he been behaving like some wingless adolescent?

"Not to say everyone might have noticed your, uh, affection for our chieftain, but you cannot mishandle her. In public or otherwise. Is that clear?" The grizzle-haired Viking waited for Tiernan to comment. What could he say but the truth?

"You are right. If this had happened in my presence in my kingdom, I would probably have skewered the man." Tiernan stood up and walked around. "It's just that Mista is so frustrating."

"Aye, I do know that." Baldr's lips pulled back in a full-toothed smile. "She has been a handful ever since her birthing day." The man frowned before continuing. "'Tis the truth, her life would have been much different if her older brother Vidar had not been kidnapped when Mista was just a baby."

Tiernan moved to sit in a chair close to the bed where Baldr perched. "Brother?"

"Baldr?" Gunhilde marched into the room, glared at Tiernan and then her husband. "You dare to bring this man to our chamber?" Her brown eyes dewed with what could have been hurt.

"Aye, woman, I have. 'Tis man talk we be discussing." Baldr didn't snarl at his wife, but his tone brooked no misunderstanding.

"And you did not think I should have something to say…about a man who could be in league with Erik. Why, he could have even killed our son!" This time there was no mistaking the tears in her voice.

"Nay, Gunhilde. It has yet to be decided if Tiernan even knew Erik before the day we found him. And I trust you not to act as if I do not care about our son's murderer." Baldr stood up and crossed to the veritable Amazon standing near the door.

"Please, woman, I love you, now let this rest. I will explain everything to you later." He dropped a kiss on Gunhilde's mouth.

She in turn gave him another glare. "See that you do, old man. Now, I will bring you some mead to quench your thirst."

A few moments later, she returned and placed a pitcher and goblets near Baldr, before returning the earlier kiss. A second later she was gone.

"I know you think I be too easy on my wife, but she has not only been my lover for over twenty years and the mother of my only child, but an excellent warrior also." The last bit was said with a proud smile as he filled the goblets to their brims.

"So she fought by your side?" Tiernan took the

goblet offered.

Baldr laughed. "Nay, I fought at hers. The woman would have it no other way. She said she wanted me close so she could protect me."

"And she is doing the same thing now with Mista." Tiernan took a sip and awaited Baldr's response.

"Aye, she has fair raised that child. Mista's mother died in childbed. It was then my wife gave up her sword to take care of the babe."

Well that explained why every time he'd seen Baldr's wife she'd given him a wide berth.

"So Mista had an older brother."

"Aye, Randver and Menja, Mista's parents, doted on the child. Vidar was four winters in age when he went to the market with Menja." Baldr's voice trembled a bit. "'Twas nothing new for him to do so, but this time he became separated from his mother and the warriors guarding him."

Tiernan took another sip of his drink and leaned forward. "What happened?"

"We never really found out for certain. One moment he was there, the next he was gone. Randver sent out scores of warriors to scour the countryside. He thought at first Vidar had been kidnapped for ransom." Baldr wiped a speck of mead off his lip. "Even back then, the Einarsson Clan was one of the strongest, most profitable clans around."

"Was Vidar kidnapped?" He held his breath, so much about Mista's reticence, prickly attitude toward men, and her almost immovable pride, could be answered.

"Nay. A note was never sent, and after six moons passed, Randver gave up any hope of seeing his son.

Menja seemed to sink into herself. She wanted nothing to do with the running of the household. The only time she behaved like her old self was when near Randver. He kept his business as close to home as possible to give Menja some peace of mind.

"This continued for almost two years, and then she discovered she was carrying Mista. We all hoped this would end her fragile mind-set, but when she gave birth and realized her husband's new heir was a daughter, she just gave up."

"Please tell me Mista's father did not feel the same." Tiernan gripped the goblet so hard he feared he would crush the stem.

"Odin's sword, nay. Randver loved Mista. There was nothing he would not do for his daughter. And she loved her da. When she could barely walk she toddled behind him whenever he left the castle." Baldr laughed. "Randver appointed guards just to make sure she came to no harm. And the older she got, the more she tried to be a son to him. Those two were closer than a sword and sheath."

"What happened to Randver?"

"Six years ago, a package arrived with a peddler. It contained the threadbare clothes Vidar had been wearing when he disappeared. Rust-colored stains covered some of the tunic, and it was as if Randver was forced to grieve all over again." Baldr slugged down the liquid in his goblet and poured another drink with a hand that shook slightly.

"But wrapped up in the leggings was a note stating Vidar was alive and well. There were instructions telling where to find him. Of course, Randver knew his son would be fully grown, and might not remember him or his heritage, but he left to find him."

Tiernan took a sip of the mead. Although he knew the outcome, the thought of losing a child, then finding hope again, only to meet death had to devastate the entire Einarsson clan. Not to mention what it would have done to Mista.

"Randver's body was discovered only a mile or so from Einarsson lands. Snow had fallen a day or so after he left, and if one of the men had not seen the flash of his sword, we would have never known what happened. That winter food was scarce, and wolves and bears roamed closer to inhabited lands more than usual.

"Mista, who had just celebrated twenty years of life, prepared the body for a Viking burial with the help of my wife. And once Randver was on his way to Valhalla, Mista took over the clan."

Before Tiernan could respond to Baldr's horrific story, Gunhilde bustled into the room. "If you men are going to spend the evening talking then at least light a lantern so a body will not trip."

He glanced toward the window. Twilight had indeed come and gone, but with the light from the hearth, neither of them had noticed.

"Here." Baldr's wife pulled a table between her husband and Tiernan, and then motioned for one of the kitchen slaves. The young girl carried in a tray almost as large as her slender frame.

"You need to eat, husband." She patted Baldr on the shoulder.

At that moment Tiernan's stomach let out a rude roar.

"See to it that this man eats also."

Gunhilde left the room and both he and Baldr begin

to fill their bellies.

Chapter Twelve

Mista stabbed at the slice of roasted venison on her plate before cutting off a miniscule bite. The meat was tender but tasted like ashes against her tongue. She finished chewing and then took a deep gulp of her mead.

Why were Tiernan and Baldr still in Baldr's chamber? What were they talking about, and how and why had her second-in-command become a confidante for Tiernan?

She had been a wellspring of anxiety ever since Baldr spirited Tiernan away. Although probably for the best, since she was certain he planned to punish her words with a kiss. And only the Christian God knew she had no idea how she would have responded.

A maid approached bearing a platter of boiled carrots and parsnips, but Mista waved her away. She did not want the food on her plate. She wanted answers. Gunhilde had been close-mouthed when she passed by Mista right before time for the evening meal. A servant followed her with a loaded tray.

"Where are you going?"

"I am taking our *náttmál* to Baldr and the slave." Her words were clipped but there did not seem to be any anger in her gaze.

"Gunhilde, do you know what they be talking of?"

"Nay, but Baldr told me he would speak of their

conversation later." Gunhilde motioned to Mora and then she was gone.

What in Hel's name could they be discussing? Mista had at first worried they would come to blows, but as much as she tried to listen from the corridor, she heard nothing but low murmurs. Now her anger rose even more sharply as the table was cleared, and her warriors prepared for bed. She needed to know what was happening. She deserved to know as chieftain.

Her mind made up Mista started for the stairs. Her stride remained firm, even though her hands where they gripped the smooth wall trembled just a bit.

Baldr's voice rumbled but she could not understand what he was saying. Mista moved closer.

"Now you know about Mista. Tell me about you."

Her mouth dropped open. Baldr had discussed her with Tiernan?

The repercussions of what Tiernan may have learned caused her stomach to clench in a vicious grip. And what had Tiernan shared with Baldr.

"Baldr!" She walked into the chamber and glared at both men. Baldr looked like an elk caught in a beam of moonlight, but Tiernan gave her a cheeky grin. She wanted to strangle both men, but would wait until she sorted this out.

"Mista, I be not expecting you." Baldr sounded startled. Good.

"Aye, I be sure you were not. Now, what is so secretive you keep it from your chieftain?" She glared at her warrior and for good measure sent another one Tiernan's way. He deserved it for causing her a sleepless night and unsettled emotions.

"'Tis nothing for you to worry about. I merely told

Tiernan about your parents and Vidar."

Mista could feel the blood leaving her face. Why would he talk about her brother? And to this man?

"Are you all right, Mista?" Tiernan spoke for the first time, but she waved off his concern.

"My family's history is not something to be shared with a stranger." She tried to rein in her temper. In her heart she knew Baldr would not normally discuss the tragic events that had taken place before she was born. And there were those, Baldr included, that felt they should not touch her heart as they did.

Yet, she had watched her da mourn since she was old enough to talk. And she had buried him because of what had happened to her brother.

"Mista, I am not a stranger and you know this." Tiernan stood and moved to her side. She stepped back, but he only closed the distance between them.

"You can never be more to me than a stranger, Tiernan. You know this and you know why." Mista almost strangled on her words as the truth assailed her again. She wanted this man to be more to her, but to do so would mean giving up all she knew if his tale of being a fae king was true. If indeed he might want her for more than one night.

"Mista, I—"

"Well, *I* do not know why, so if you would sit down, then Tiernan can tell me." Baldr stared at Mista until she sat down next to him on the bed.

The Viking then nodded at Tiernan. His stomach was in a knot. Would Baldr believe him?

"I only know of one way to tell you about me and where I come from. After I finish, then ask me anything you like." He took another sip of mead, swallowed the drink, and then caught Baldr's gaze with his own.

"I know you believe in a realm where your Norse gods live. I come from a world that is also in an alternate universe."

"Universe?" Baldr's question wasn't so much disbelieving as curious.

"Yes, a world where certain people live, but they are not visible to others." He took a deep breath. "Like you believe in Asgard, and Mista believes in Heaven. Neither one of you can see it, but you both accept these places are real."

Baldr picked up his goblet and took several deep swallows. "Aye, I have not seen Asgard, but was taught that it resides in a place that only the gods can see."

Mista remained silent.

"My world is a world of magick. My people are immortal and almost as old as time itself. We keep to ourselves with no mortal contact, or we did until my daughter, Catriona, chose to meddle in mortal matters."

Tiernan's thoughts veered to his oldest child. He hoped she was well, and Willamina had not tried any of her magick on Cat or her husband. He was grateful that Celine, his youngest and her husband, were off on an extended vacation.

"You know magick?" Baldr leaned forward, his brown eyes wide, and his gaze was filled with excitement if Tiernan was correct.

"I do, but as I told Mista, because my daughter married a mortal, and I allowed her to break our laws in order to do so, she would have been punished."

"And you took the punishment yourself as any father would do."

"Yes, Baldr, and that is why I am in a century that

is so far behind the one I left."

"How long is your sentence?"

"A year."

Baldr stood and begin to pace. "And then you will return home." His statement brought to the surface what Tiernan desired and feared.

"Yes, but I don't want to leave Mista behind."

"Nay, I could not go with you if I wanted to." Mista looked horrified.

"Why? You know I care for you. Could you not be happy in my world?"

"I cannot leave my clan. I am their chieftain." She too stood up and began to pace.

"Mista, you know that if you were to leave, I will be honored to act in your place." Baldr caught her arm while Tiernan stayed seated. He wasn't sure if he could stand anyway. He knew Mista had doubts about him, but…

"Are you telling me you believe his tale?" The arm Baldr held trembled.

"It makes as much sense as some of the other things I have heard in my lifetime. Besides, he can prove his claim by doing magick."

"That's just it, Baldr. I can't. When I was sent back in time, I was banned from using my magick." Tiernan watched Mista and her second-in-command.

"Why?" Baldr looked more than a bit puzzled.

"Because of a jealous woman. Willamina is very much like Erik Runolfsson. She wants what is not hers to have. She put that edict in, and if I use my magick I will lose it forever."

"And that is not all, Baldr." Mista looked miserable. "If Tiernan uses his magick he will also lose his ability to bed a woman."

Baldr's gasp echoed in the sudden silence of the chamber. His eyes resembled small marbles in their display of horror.

"Now you know why I cannot prove my claim." Tiernan sat back down.

"'Tis quite a tale you have told, Tiernan." Baldr rubbed a hand over his face. "And aye, I believe all of it. No man would make up such a tale. 'Twould be like putting a curse on his manhood if it were not true."

Tiernan shook the hand Baldr held out, and then turned to Mista.

"Mista, could we talk?"

"There is nothing to speak about. My life is here, yours is in a faraway land." Her eyes were clear, and he wondered if her decision affected her heart in any way at all.

"Now, I have duties to see to. I suggest you both get some rest." Without another word, Mista left the room.

****

For the second night in a row, Tiernan eased open the door of Mista's chamber. Unlike the night before, the room was pitch-black. Not even a fire had been lit. His gaze scoured the room and found what he sought.

Mista lay on the bed. Her body covered with several coverlets, her head cradled on one arm. He crept closer. Her dark lashes were weighed down with moisture, her cheeks pink from crying.

If only he could have prevented her hurt. Yet, to deny his feelings for her would be like denying his magick. Tiernan longed to take her in his arms and love her, but not tonight. Tonight he would just hold her.

He stripped off his clothes, folded them, and placed them on a trunk. The sheets felt like ice against his skin when he slid in next to Mista. His hand encountered what felt like wool material. He hated wool, but it was warm. Tiernan pulled the sleeping armful close.

The press of her buttocks against his groin caused heat of a different kind to build inside his body. He pulled her closer. Mista raised her head and struggled against him.

"Shush, Mista. I only plan to hold you. Nothing more." His voice rumbled out in a whisper of frustration and lust. Yes, he wanted her, but not like a thief in the night, nor as a cause of her grief.

A small sniffle, a slight hitch in her breath, and then Mista was asleep once more. However dawn stretched across the horizon before Tiernan fell into his own slumber.

****

Tiernan awoke alone. The bed was even colder, his body freezing, and Mista nowhere to be found. He wanted to pull off his wings. The woman had bolted again. He squinted his eyes against the sunlight coming in through the window. At least it wasn't snowing, but by now Baldr would have missed him on the practice field.

Once dressed, he ran down the stairs and then came to a complete stop.

Mista sat in her place at the high table, dressed in warrior garb, Baldr by her side. Another Viking stood across the table from them. Baldr spotted Tiernan first, and leaned over to whisper something in Mista's ear. A second later, she motioned him forward.

"We have news that should make you extremely

happy." She smiled but only with a twist of her lips. Her blue gaze looked haunted.

"About?" Tiernan wanted to go to her, pull the little chieftain into his arms. To ask her why she'd left him alone in her bed. He did none of those.

"Olav has been to Erik's holdings. He spent several days there." She motioned to the younger Viking. "He will tell you what he found."

Olav cleared his throat. "I made my way to Runolfsson's clan. Once there I worked as a blacksmith and by listening during meals and to those who needed their horses shod, I found out two things."

Puzzled, Tiernan waited for the man to get to whatever he was trying to say.

Mista motioned for Olav to continue.

"This man, Tiernan, is not part of Erik's group."

Tiernan couldn't believe after these last few days that Mista would still think he had anything to do with her enemy.

"So, you thought I lied about who I was?"

"Tiernan, you must understand I had to know for certain. I could not take a chance that you might be involved." Her words made sense to the king in him, but his heart did not want to hear them.

"I see. So how can you believe Olav when you didn't believe me?"

"Olav has no reason to tell me anything but the truth." Mista waved her hand at Olav. "What else did you find out?"

"That Chieftain Runolfsson plans another attack."

Despite the brevity of Olav's words, Mista smiled.

"Does he? Well, we will be ready when he comes. Thank you, Olav. Have something to eat and then rest for a bit before you go to the practice field."

Olav walked away toward the kitchen.

"I take it, since my innocence has been proven, you will take this collar off of me?" Tiernan queried.

"Yes, see the blacksmith and he will remove it." Mista said nothing else, but stood to her feet. She was leaving just like that—not even a hint of his care of her the night before apparent. Not a smidgen of affection in her gaze.

"Hold, Mista. We have unfinished business."

Chapter Thirteen

Tiernan skirted the high table, nodded once at Baldr, and barred Mista's escape route.

"I believe we have covered everything. Now if you will excuse me, I want to make sure our men are apprised of Erik's upcoming attack." She made a move to go around him, and he grabbed her arm.

"Let me go." Her hiss echoed somewhere near his chest as he pulled her into his body.

"I don't think so. I am no longer a slave." He looked at Baldr, "Isn't that right?"

"Aye. So I will be leaving you two to settle matters between yourselves." His grin caused a twin smile from Tiernan, but another reaction entirely from Mista.

"Baldr, you will go nowhere. Is that understood?"

"Mista, I love you as my own daughter, but this is not something I will involve myself in. If I feared he would hurt you, then yes, but he will not." Baldr stepped off the dais and left.

"Tiernan, you may not be a slave, but it is still against the law to touch a woman against her will."

Her words shocked Tiernan so much he dropped his arms. Mista in turn backed away.

"I have never touched a woman without her consent, but you are trying me to no patience." Tiernan advanced, and Mista had no place to go. Her back was up against the hall's wall.

"Now, I suggest you come with me so we can talk or I will be forced to do something I would rather not do."

Mista snarled at him, and he couldn't decide to applaud her foolishness or drag her over his shoulder right then and there.

"Snarling is not becoming to a chieftain of your clan, Mista. Perhaps we could speak as one leader to another?" He hoped she would agree, but...

"I stand by what I said before. We have nothing more to say to one another." She peered up at him, and the flash of defiance in her eyes barely hid what looked like pain.

Did the thought of his leaving affect Mista as it was affecting him? He needed to talk to her, but the stubborn woman would fight him every inch of the way. So be it!

Mista gasped when Tiernan grabbed her arm, and unceremoniously tossed her over one broad shoulder. Her fists struck muscle as hard as a winter's freeze. The band across her upper thighs tightened.

"Stop, Mista. I warned you, now you will behave."

Her head bounced against the softness of his tunic as he stepped off the dais. She heard the exclamations of servants as he walked through the hall and to the stairs. Mista felt like a slingshot as her entire body was forced to comply with his rapid steps.

She fought the urge to retch when she became dizzy and then Tiernan's stride lengthened. A moment more, and she heard the creak of a door opening. Before she could even draw in another breath her body was airborne. She hit the mattress on her bed—hard. Her breath escaped in little puffs of air. Before she could regroup he was on her.

His blue eyes burned with a flame of a warrior. She'd not truly doubted he was one, she knew that from his fight with Magnor, but for the first time, she felt uneasy. The ice she glimpsed behind the flame reminded her of a berserker. A Viking gone mad with bloodlust and killing. Mista prayed Tiernan had control over the beast lurking within him.

"Tiernan?"

"Do not speak—not yet." He moved away from her prone body, and secured the door. Now no one could get in unless they broke the door down. And that would take several of her strongest warriors with battle-axes. She'd best see if she could reason with him, but perhaps she would wait a bit longer.

After pacing several times around her chamber, Tiernan finally poured a goblet of water, raised it to his lips, and quaffed the entire contents. Again he paced.

Mista did not believe or she prayed he truly would not do her harm, but just in case she edged an inch or so over toward the side of the bed. She always kept a dagger under the bottom lip of the mattress.

Tiernan turned toward the window. His gaze not quite as fiery as before, but the vacant look disturbed her. Another few inches and she would be able to slide her hand to grasp the dagger. Her fingers crept slowly toward their goal, still keeping her eyes on Tiernan. She choked back a sigh of relief when she touched the slightly rough hilt of her weapon.

Slowly and with extreme caution, she palmed the knife. Tiernan still looked out the window. Carefully as if she were handling a newborn babe, she lifted and then slid the blade under her upper thigh. 'Twould be better if she could have placed it on her right side, but she would have to take her chances using her left hand if Tiernan gave her no choice.

"Mista." His voice boomed in the silence of the room. Had he seen her furtive attempts?

"Yes?" She hoped her tone did not give away the fact she was just a scant hair from going berserk with nerves.

"It is time you came to a decision." Although his tone was softer, it still caused a wedge of chill to coat her spine.

"About what?" She tried to deliver her question in a clipped voice. No need to allow him to see she was anything but a self-assured chieftain.

"Us."

That one word frightened Mista more than a group of berserking Vikings. There could be no "us"—she could not leave her people—not without a chieftain— especially now with Erik's impending attack.

"Tiernan, I am not sure what you want from me. I told you, you were free to go. There is nothing else I can do."

"I have told you, I don't want to leave without you." He finally looked her way. The blue in his eyes a faint remnant of before.

"We both know you have no choice. When your sentence is over you have to return to your land. You have to protect *your* people." Mista sat up cross-legged on the bed.

"Come with me." He did not beg, but she heard just a slight tremble in his words.

She jumped off the bed, and the blade fell to the floor, its clamor sounding like thunder.

Although Tiernan knew she could and probably would have protected herself if he'd touched her in anger, he ignored the weapon. If she'd wanted to use it on him, she would have. He stood silent—waiting for her response.

"You know I cannot do that. I cannot leave my home, my people." Mista caught his gaze with her own, but then much to his regret, she looked away. "There is no one else. Perhaps if my brother..."

The tears coating her lashes melted his anger and to some extent his frustration with her and the situation.

"Don't cry. Somehow we will make it work." His words sounded like he meant them but inside his heart ached. To give up the people he'd governed for millennia or to give up his second chance at love were two choices he did not want to make.

"How? You can't stay, and I cannot go." She closed the distance between them. Her hand touched his face, and the caress she bestowed on him felt like a gentle but melancholy raindrop.

"We *will* figure it out. Right now, I just want to hold you." Tiernan dipped his head and caught her trembling lips with his own.

The touch of her softness stole his breath. So innocent, yet so strong. He wanted to take her away, to keep her safe, to tie her to him forever.

Her lips parted, and he tasted the sweetness of the mead she'd drunk earlier. He wanted to drown in her essence, but he also wanted more. He could make love to Mista, but if she would not leave with him, could he bear to have her for a short time, and then live with the barrenness of having lost her?

"Tiernan?" Her whisper brought him back from his

what-ifs. His answer was to take her mouth more fully, to vanquish the heartache by branding every inch of her mouth with his touch. And he didn't stop there. His hands slid down to pluck the ties loose from her tunic top, even as he kept his lips on hers, and to cup the soft flesh hidden beneath the material.

Her sigh echoed against his lips and heated his body to a fast-rising temperature. His touch became more possessive, but Mista didn't stop him. He brought the reddened tips of her breasts to his mouth and suckled like a babe lapping a mother's milk.

Her hands caught his hair and tugged lightly. He pulled her closer into his body, and then lifted her off the floor. Her legs locked around his hips, and her center aligned with his arousal. Faery wings! He was ready to explode with passion, and they were still clothed.

Thoughts of getting Mista naked overcame his rationale on not making love to her and possibly leaving her pregnant. He wanted her, needed her, and he would have her.

His hand moved to untie the string of her leggings, and he slid his hand down to caress the warmth between her thighs. Tiernan bit back a shout when he found Mista hot, wet, and ready for him.

"Tiernan?" Her blue gaze looked confused but her pupils began to dilate as he widened his exploration.

"It's all right, I will make it better." His voice was hoarse with his own need, and the need to see to his woman. For that was what Mista was. Never, since the death of his beloved wife, had he felt this way about another female. He wanted to possess all of her, to wrap her up inside himself and keep her safe forever.

Her ankles gripped his buttocks, as he stroked her warm flesh. Her lower body thrust gently at first and then harder against the part of him aching to sheath itself inside of Mista. He moved to the bed and eased them down on it—the movement brought her sex even closer to his shaft.

"Mista, you are killing me." His words came out on a groan.

"Then you best do something about it." Her soft whisper was edged with laughter, but her eyes fairly gleamed with desire.

In one swift upsweep, he divested her of the tunic. The nipples he'd palmed into crests hardened more in the cool air.

His hands trembled slightly, and were clumsy as he finished unlacing her leggings, pulled off her soft boots, and then those items also found a place on the floor. For a moment, he just stared at the beauty before him. Tiernan's eyes burned with emotion. Mista, who'd never known a man's touch, would willingly give him what no other had claimed.

His hand touched the downy reddish-blonde curls hiding her womanhood, and Mista inhaled sharply. Her hips rose off the mattress, pushing against his palm. He increased the pressure of his caress, and then slid his fingers past her nether lips to lightly pinch the nub resting within.

"Tiernan..."

He welcomed her gasp of pleasure, and sought to bring her more. His hand moved faster, the friction of her lower body thrusting against his palm and in doing so against his own arousal turned that part of him into concrete. Yet, he did not want to take her completely until she experienced her own release. He wanted his possession to be pain free as possible for Mista.

Her buttocks twisted, and her breath came in spasms of air as she moved harder—faster—as did Tiernan. He bent to take her right nipple in his mouth. The way Mista responded to him made Tiernan feel as if he were with his first woman. And although it had been a long time since he'd made love, he would not shame himself or Mista by coming before her.

Tiernan tongued her left nipple and then closed his mouth over her parted lips. His hand slid toward the apex of his desire. One finger explored and then pushed gently against the flesh signifying her virginal status. Mista flinched slightly as he broke through the barrier. He buried his finger deeper, and she rotated her hips around the digit. He added a second and then third finger to find the one spot that would trigger her falling over the edge.

He felt the hum of her desire and then in one swift move he pushed against her pleasure spot. Mista's frame completely left the bed as her body undulated with the paroxysm of fulfillment. After several moments, she lay still and he removed his mouth from hers.

When he did so, Mista caught his arm. "You be not leaving are you?" The out of breath question made him smile.

"No, there is so much more we will explore, my love." Tiernan eased down on the bed beside her, and his hand caressed the soft skin right above her mons. "Much, much—"

"Chieftain, you are needed downstairs." The overloud voice of one of her warriors jarred Mista from her post-climatic stupor.

"Olav, where is Baldr?" Mista gave Tiernan a regretful smile. Thor's thunder, she did not want to leave her chamber, or him. He'd shown her such pleasure she had feared to die from it, but she knew enough of men to know he too needed release. Yet, Olav would not have come to her chamber unless something was amiss.

"He is entertaining a visitor at the door." The young Viking's voice sounded strangled. Could he be in danger? What of the keep? Her clan?

"I will be there in a moment." She pushed away from the warmth of Tiernan's body, and struggled into her clothes. She pulled on her boots, and raked a hand through her disheveled hair.

"Here, you might need this." Tiernan handed her the blade that had fallen to the floor. His smile tugged at her heart. She wondered if he hated the interruption as much as she did.

"Thank you. I will return as quickly as I can." Mista hastened to the door.

"I am coming with you." His words brooked no argument, and she found she didn't want one. She would welcome this man at her side as long as she could keep him.

"Thank you."

Together they exited the room, and their boots made haste of the stairs as they followed Olav downward.

The sight that met Mista's eyes when she arrived in the hall was one of confusion. Baldr stood with Magnor who did not look at all pleased.

"Magnor, we were not expecting you." She forced

a smile past her numb lips. Her body still experiencing aftershocks of her explosive time with Tiernan.

"Aye, and I was not expecting the greeting I received from your second-in-command." Magnor looked past Mista and spotted Tiernan.

"What? You now allow slaves to roam the halls of your keep?" His slur on Tiernan made her want to slap his twisted lips.

"Tiernan is no longer a slave." Mista moved forward and then with an outstretched arm signaled Baldr to step back.

"He wears a collar." Magnor closed the distance between them and grasped her arm.

A growl exploded from behind her. She turned to face Tiernan. She caught his hand, then stood on her tiptoes. He leaned down, and she whispered, "Please, allow me to handle this." A terse nod of his head was her answer, but the kiss he placed on her hand encompassed her in warmth and need.

"Magnor, please have a seat, and Tiernan's collar will be removed." She looked to Baldr who motioned Tiernan to follow him. At least now she had her two staunchest supporters out of the room. She caught the eye of one of the women servants. "Bethenia, please bring some mead for our guest." She turned to Magnor. "Have you eaten this eve?"

"Aye, but thank you." Magnor's smile seemed genuine, but forced. Why in the Christian God's Heaven was he here?

Once they were sipping mead she asked him, "So what do I owe the pleasure of your visit, Magnor?"

He took another sip and then cleared his throat. "I wanted to apologize to you. I feel that my last visit might have caused you some consternation."

Mista quelled the disdainful laughter threatening to spill forth. Magnor had never cared if he caused anyone any problems. He wanted something or else he would not be here now. She needed to find out what.

Chapter Fourteen

"What in the hell are you doing sitting on my da's throne?" Catriona, Tiernan's oldest daughter and his heir marched toward Willamina.

Willamina, a prudent faery when it came to self-preservation, backed up. "It is good to see you again, Catriona. How are things in mortal land?" She smiled and employed all her faculties to pull off a faery-may-care attitude. She needed to snow the little fae into thinking all was well. That daddy dearest was safe as he would be if he was back at the court. Not! "And how is your husband?"

"My husband is none of your business, Willamina. Now, where is my da?" The younger faery's green eyes flashed emerald, a sure sign she was a tad upset. Time to diffuse the little mortal-lover. This would not be easy; Catriona took after Tiernan in intelligence and tenacity.

"Your dear da has taken a sabbatical."

"Liar." Catriona stalked closer. "He would not leave without letting me know."

Willamina wished she could spell the girl, but being Tiernan's daughter, she was as powerful as Willamina.

"Oh but he did. And I'm sure he would have told you but a man does not like to talk about intimate trysts with his children." She watched as Catriona's face twisted in a grimace before she silently high-fived herself.

"Fine, Da is entitled to company. He's been a widower for a long time. I'm just surprised you know so much about this." She raked a hand through hair the color of moonbeams. Quite a contrast from Willamina's own dark tresses. She envied the younger faery her looks, her youth, and above else her place in Tiernan's court and heart.

"Well, he felt it prudent to confide in someone, so I guess I was the lucky recipient."

"Still, I'm surprised that you are here. Surely you are not trying to govern the court yourself?" Catriona's question stung like a whip. The insolent child actually thought she, Willamina, one of the oldest, most beautiful fae to ever exist, was incompetent.

"Of course I am. Your da gave me carte blanche." She practically purred the last word.

"I don't believe you. None of this makes sense. And mark my words, Willamina, I will find out the truth—one way or the other." Catriona didn't shout her accusation or threat, but the soft way she uttered her words caused a chill to feather along Willamina's spine. Before she could appease the woman or deny her claims, Catriona disappeared without a trace, without even uttering a teleportation spell or lifting her hand.

Tiernan's daughter had indeed grown in strength. She would bear watching. Willamina stood and began to pace. Tiernan was out of the picture, but she needed to find a way to shut down Catriona. The bumbling male trio, Alex, Jared, and Gideon, could not be allowed to speak with Tiernan's heir. If they did, she had no doubt they would once again question what had happened on the day of Tiernan's sentencing.

The past week had been quiet. She'd enjoyed redecorating the castle to suit her needs. She had taken overabundant joy at zapping the remainder of lights from Catriona's wedding. And even though Catriona had not remarked on the palace, ablaze with crimson and gold tones, she would not hesitate to change everything back to where it was once Tiernan returned. Which should not happen for almost twelve months.

In the meantime, she needed to cover her wings on how to get Catriona to leave off her queries about Tiernan's disappearance. And to keep the male fae from divining her network of lies.

****

Tiernan could have levitated with glee when the collar came off. "Thank you, Baldr."

"You be welcome, Tiernan. Fact is, I am glad to have this done with also. It makes it easier for the men to treat you even more as an equal. Not to mention, if you do plan to court Mista, no one can toss your slave status into the mix." Baldr chuckled. "Not that I think either you or Mista would pay much heed to what others say."

"Myself, no, but Mista's chieftainship must not be challenged because of her relationship with me."

"Then you have decided to stay?" Baldr's stare was a bit incredulous.

"For the time being at least. I can't go anyway before my sentence expires or I will lose my magic. I don't want that to happen."

"So your court peers would punish you if you magicked yourself back to your time and place?" Baldr's gaze turned puzzled.

"No, not the men on the court, but once my magick is gone, only by assenting votes from all the council members, excluding myself can it be restored."

Tiernan prayed it would not come to that. Willamina would never vote yes, and that left him with only two options. To stay here with Mista until his sentence was up, or to try and find the time portal he came through in. But even if he did, that would not mean he could go back the same way.

"Then what be the problem?"

"A woman—or faery—named Willamina." He sighed. "She's been trying to get her wings into me since my wife died centuries ago. I don't want her and do not intend to have her. This is her way of punishing me."

"Aye, women can be vindictive even if they are not mortal." Baldr gave him a commiserating look before asking, "Why do you think Magnor is back?"

"To soothe things with Mista. Why he's doing it, I don't know. I thought it was just him pulling rank over a slave when we fought, but I think it is more." Tiernan looked the Viking in the eye. "I think he wants Mista for his wife, and even though his technique is more civilized than Erik's when it comes to courting, I believe he will be more than a bit upset when she turns him down."

Baldr smirked. "And you are sure she will?"

Tiernan grinned. "Oh yes, more than sure. Now I suggest we get back to the hall. I don't trust the man as far as I can throw him."

The older man slapped Tiernan on the back. "Aye, on that we are in agreement."

They arrived back in time to see Magnor raise his

goblet. "To the most beautiful woman in Norseland."

Mista's cheeks turned pink as she looked away from Magnor. Her gaze found Tiernan, and he smiled as he thought of how he would love to see that lovely shade of color encompass her entire body. And he would be the one to put it there.

"Tiernan, Baldr, please join us." Mista waved them over to the dais. "Magnor, you of course know Baldr, but allow me to introduce Tiernan with his rightful title." She picked up her goblet and held it for a moment before continuing.

"When we found him he was unconscious and due to circumstances we assumed he was from the Runolfsson clan. However, his home is quite a bit farther than Erik's keep. Tiernan is actually king of the Seelie Court."

Magnor's mouth fell open, but then a second later he recovered. "I have never heard of such a place."

"Neither had we, but his tale is true. So why don't we all put the past behind us and start anew?"

Tiernan sat down next to Mista and Baldr sat next to him. He ignored the frown Magnor displayed and caught Mista's hand in his. No words were spoken but he knew she was thinking of their earlier encounter. He hoped she looked forward to their next one as much as he did.

****

Conversation was next to nil. Magnor was sullen, Tiernan unbelievably charming and tender with his quiet touches on her arm, and Baldr sat as a rock—never voicing any type of comment. Whereas Mista wanted nothing more than to retire to her chamber in hope Tiernan would join her. The magick he'd wrought on her body earlier had been unbelievable. She could not wait to know how it would be when they were truly joined as a man and woman.

"Magnor, Bethenia will show you to your chamber. I hope that you rest well." Mista stood and so did the men on either side of her. She gave Magnor a small smile, and then froze when he grasped her hand.

"Mista, I want you to consider what an alliance would mean between our two clans. A marriage between you and I would cement the friendship our fathers shared." His gaze was earnest, but something else lurked in his eyes. She would like to know what, but for right now she would answer him.

"Magnor, I too cherish the friendship of our clans, and I want it to be something that will be shared by our future clansmen years from now." Mista gently withdrew her hand from his. "However, I cannot marry you."

"Can't or won't?" The almost congenial man of a moment before disappeared.

"Both. I do not love you, and I have no plans to marry anyone at the moment." She heard the growl Tiernan issued, and was mildly surprised he'd held it in for this long.

"And this is neither the time nor place to discuss the topic any longer. The day has been long, and we all need to rest. We will talk in the morning." Mista motioned again to the maid. "Please show our guest to a sleeping chamber."

Knowing it would do no good to say anything else to any of the three men frowning ardently at her, she stepped off the dais and made for her chamber. If Tiernan followed all the better, but if not... Well it would not be the first or the last time she spent the night alone. Her steps were a bit heavy as she canvassed the stairs, but when she reached the landing above she heard a second pair.

Mista turned, hoping against all that was mortal that Magnor was not the one behind her. Her breath swelled out in an *oomph* when Tiernan picked her up in his arms and carried her to her chamber. The look on his face was not angry—instead he wore his stone face, making it hard for her to know what he thought.

He set her gently on her feet, closed the door, and stood there staring at her. Mista felt like a fish waiting to be skinned.

"All right, tell me what's on your mind, Tiernan." Better to take the offense then try to defend her actions. Not that she had any reason to; she behaved as any chieftain would have under the same circumstances.

"I don't trust Magnor." His gaze was direct, his manner non-threatening, but she could sense the anger beneath.

"Please, it has been a stressful day in several ways." Mista moved to a chair, and toed off her boots. "It is late, Tiernan, and although I am in agreement Magnor bears watching, he did come alone."

She placed her boots next to the chair and stood. "I think we can address anything else in the morning. I am sure he will be leaving."

"Because you turned his marriage offer down?" Tiernan moved to stand in front of her.

"Yes. What reason would he have for staying?" She noticed the lines fanning around his eyes. He looked tired. And she felt the same. The exhilaration of their interrupted lovemaking had been eclipsed by the tension filled night.

"Mista, that man is not going to just go away. He will try to sway your decision."

"How do you know this? You do not even know Magnor that well." She rubbed her arms and then sighed.

"Because I am a man. And I know I would not give up, and I believe you already know that." He sounded smug, but also a bit worn. Was he tired of trying to convince her to leave with him? Would he leave without her when he could?

"All right, Magnor will not stop, but can we not wait until morning before having to confront him?" She sat on the bed. "I'm tired. I just want to rest."

Tiernan looked closely at Mista's features. She did indeed look worn-out. Her porcelain skin looked more iridescent. Her blue eyes did not shine as they had when he'd introduced her to their partial lovemaking. There were faint shadows under her lower lashes, and her shoulders were not as straight in stance.

"Very well. Get some sleep. Tomorrow we will take care of Magnor."

"We?" Her expression was a bit quizzical but also hopeful.

"Yes, love. As long as I am here, you do not have to fight alone against anything or anyone." Tiernan sat down also and pulled her close to his side.

Chapter Fifteen

Tiernan and Mista awoke to sounds of shouts and cries of pain. They had fallen asleep fully clothed except for their shoes, holding one another. Now as one unit they rolled off the bed. Mista crouched at an old chest near the bed, grabbed her weapons, and then pulled out a sword and tossed it to him.

"Someone must have breached our walls." Mista looked half-asleep, but her features quickly hardened into anger. "I need to see whom and what damage they have done to our people."

She ran to the chamber door and started to pull it open, but Tiernan stopped her. "You don't know who is right outside."

"It does not matter. I have to fight." The gaze she gave him was filled with desperation.

"Yes, we will both fight. I will go first. They would expect you and not me." Tiernan placed his hand over hers on the latch. The argument he expected did not happen.

Mista stepped back, raised her weapon, and nodded her head.

He pushed the latch up and then eased the door open. To any who might be lurking outside, they would expect the chieftain to rush from her chamber. Tiernan wanted to catch them off guard.

When the corridor proved to be empty, both he and

Mista ran to the landing. Smoke burped upward in gentle puffs, which meant any fires started were not yet out of control, but it did not set his mind at ease. They did not know how many warriors were engaged in battle with Mista's clan.

The cries grew louder, and through the chaos Baldr's voice echoed. "Ye sorry piece of dirt. Is this how ye repay Mista's kindness?"

Tiernan did not hear the other man's reply, but wasted no time in hurrying down the stairs—Mista so close on his heels she almost passed him. He drew to a stop and surveyed the great room.

Wounded men lay in pools of blood, while others fought with deadly menace. Servants were slapping at the small fires and for the most part were successful in keeping them from spreading. Baldr, not to Tiernan's surprise, fended off Magnor. Olav, with his back against the wall, fought two Vikings.

"Oh merciful God." Mista's gasp kept Tiernan from rushing forward.

"What is it?" He had to shout his question over the din of swords and battle-axes clanging together.

"Erik and his men are here. And the only way they could have entered inside our gates is if someone let them in."

"And that someone seems to have been Magnor." Tiernan's tone was calm, but inside he burned with a rage that required him to draw blood. He knew Mista felt the same, but he wanted her safe.

"Come, we will fight, but back to back. I don't want anything to happen to you." His words were thrown back at him.

"Aye, likewise." Mista moved into the fray of

warring Vikings, and this time Tiernan rode her heels.

****

Willamina spewed out the sip of ambrosia she'd just taken when Alex, Jared, and Gideon materialized right in front of her. A mere second later, Catriona also arrived. Stars and moons, why couldn't they leave her alone? Ever since Catriona's visit the day before, she'd been plagued with summons from all three of the male fae. Summons she had ignored.

"Have you forgotten the niceties of manners?" She hoped by going on the offensive she could deter them for as long as it took to come up with something that would prevent her from getting her wings plucked.

"You should talk about manners, Willamina." Catriona advanced toward the throne. A floor-length gossamer gown, the colors of a peacock's tail, now replaced the mortal garb she'd worn yesterday. Her hair was swept up on top of her head, and held steady by a silver-and-diamond tiara signifying her status as a royal princess. She would love to rip the crown from Catriona's head, and then tear the woman wing to wing. If she wasn't careful the royal pain-in-the-faery would ruin all her plans.

"Whatever do you mean, dear Catriona?" She sat the cup down, and then blotted the drops off the material of her gown.

"Something isn't right, and we are holding a requiem to find out just what you've done." The words fell from the younger faery's lips, and momentarily froze Willamina. If a requiem was held then she could be forced to own up to her part in Tiernan's disappearance. Then all the facts of how she switched the judgment orb, how she threatened to take away his magick, and then sent him back in time would come to light.

"Now, now, there isn't any reason to do any of that. I told you what your father said."

"Yes, and you told us something else, Willamina." Alex's baritone barked the statement and drove home the fact she'd told so many different stories she was well and truly caught. Surely there was a way out of this.

"Perhaps, I—"

"No perhaps to it. You have lied and in one hour there will be a requiem to find out what is going on." Catriona moved in so close, Willamina jerked back. How dare the insolent, spoiled brat threaten her? She could not wait to use the orb to get rid of Tiernan's offspring.

"And just so you are aware, if found guilty you will be sentenced on the spot." The princess faery's features were ice-cold as she uttered her words.

"Sentenced? For what? What have I done?" Willamina pushed to her feet, forcing Catriona to step back or be stepped on. "I am only doing what our king asked." She turned her back, pinched her arm viciously, and then showed them a face with tear-laded eyes.

"Maybe..." Gideon's sentence trailed off when Catriona turned on him.

"Maybe nothing, Uncle Gideon."

Oh how she hated the familiar relationship Tiernan and his daughters shared with the other members of the council.

"Catriona, do not worry, we will get to the bottom of this." Jared spoke up and then the other two fae nodded their heads.

"Good, because we both know my da is not and has not been with me. This witch has also told me my da had a tryst with a woman." Catriona stalked forward as she continued. "And if that is so, he would have told someone besides *her* his intentions."

The princess moved closer to the men. "And for all the faery wings in the immortal world, why on earth would you punish him for my supposed crime?"

"Now, Catriona, you know your da set up these rules, and we have been upholding them for millennia." Alex held up his hand when Tiernan's daughter opened her mouth. "Yes, some are archaic in this day and time, but until they are changed they have to be followed. Your da chose to take your punishment because he loved you, and was happy you found a love like he had with your mother—as are we. But regardless of how the rules work, we will find out where he is now." The glance he shot Willamina almost singed her unopened wings.

"Fine, then we will adjourn and meet back here in one hour." Catriona spat back.

Knowing she had no choice, Willamina waved her hand and allowed her magick to whisk her away from the fearsome foursome. She needed to get the real orb and then hide it so she could use it on the council and that little twit. If the spell was done right she could make them all forget everything and they would believe anything that came out of her mouth. Her laughter coated the air as she headed to the remote part of the universe where the Judgment Orb rested.

****

Mista's breath came in accelerated pants. She was covered in the blood of her enemies as well as blood from a few cuts to her own body. Tiernan still fought at her back, and after hazarding a glance at him, she knew he too suffered from the extended battle in which they were engaged.

It seemed like only a few moments since they awoke to the cries of battle, but now the sun spiraled in weak awakening against the horizon. Her warriors and the enemy of her clan were well-paired, but it made the battle more intense, the carnage equally horrid, and the pull on all those who fought a tremendous physical burden.

Yet, she would fight to her dying breath. As much as she loathed being in the vicinity of Erik, she wanted his head. But the warrior was elusive; he always fought close and then disappeared before she could strike. The men who stood between her and the Runolfsson chieftain seemed bent on keeping her from him.

The floors around her were coated in blood, her men's and Erik's. She just prayed to all who listened that her warriors would not be riding to Valhalla or the Christian Heaven tonight. She loved them all, and they were as loyal to her as they had been to her da.

"Mista, look out!" Tiernan's voice pulled her back into the midst of the battle. Magnor danced closer to her, his hair a black mass etched with drops of blood. His brown eyes were slitted against the sweat dripping down his forehead. His sword raised and ready to slice Mista in half.

"I see you have finally decided to grace me with your presence." Mista taunted her enemy.

Magnor who had given her a look when she and Tiernan first entered the battle had also stayed away from Mista. Now, perhaps, he felt she was weak enough he could defeat her.

"And I see you still have the slave at your feet."

Magnor's sneer had Mista bringing her sword to bear against his. The clang of metal an almost silent sound in the din of all the swords being struck.

"Fight or die, Magnor. Or just die." Mista pulled her sword back and sliced a groove of blood down her opponent's chest. She reveled in his look of disbelief and pain.

"You daughter of a bit—"

Mista cut off his aspersion on her mother. "No one talks about my mother that way." She attacked again, this time splintering the bones in his sword arm. The blood boiled up and tendons, bits of bone, and gore oozed out.

Magnor dropped his weapon, and then fell to his knees. Mista spared not a glance of pity as she ran her bloodied blade though his heart. His body would be sent back to his people, non-deserving of a warrior's burial. She would make sure his clan knew he'd dishonored the code of hospitality they prized.

The battle around them began to wane, and she was more than happy to see her men gaining the upper ground. But there was still one task she must finish.

Chapter Sixteen

Tiernan's heart rejoined the rest of his body when Magnor died, but the impulse to kill the Viking again hovered within every fiber of his being. He wanted to deliver the death-blow, but to do so would have cheated Mista from the justice she enacted on behalf of her clan. As a leader he understood this, but as the one who loved her, he hated the laws that compelled them to act in certain ways.

Instead of pulling Mista into his arms in relief that she was unharmed, he followed as she advanced slowly through the throng of warriors to get closer to Erik. Now there was a man he wanted to kill, and badly. Yet, if the chieftain had not pursued Mista in the first place, then Tiernan might not have fallen into the skirmish between their clans. And he might never have met the one woman since his wife who matched him in spirit.

"Erik!" Mista's cry echoed over the battle-weary warriors, but one in particular jerked his head toward the sound. Erik's white-blond locks were coated with the sweat of his bloody labor, and his green eyes flashed with malice as he turned back to the Einarsson Viking he had penned. A quick thrust of his sword, and the man died.

Tiernan could feel Mista's rage and despair. She loved her men as any leader should, and Erik would have much to answer for before he met death.

After wiping his blade on the dead man's tunic, Erik walked almost jauntily toward Mista and Tiernan. The smirk on his lips matched the satisfaction glowing from his gaze.

"So, Mista, we do meet again."

"Not for long, Erik. You have much to answer for. You invaded my land, stolen into my home, and all for what? Because I would not marry you? 'Tis not a worthy trait and one you certainly must have inherited from your father.

"Leave my father out of this. You had your chance to be my wife, to join our clans as both our parents wanted, but you chose not to do your duty." He spit the words out into the now silent room.

Tiernan glanced around. The recent combatants stood in small groups. He was happy to see most of the ones standing were Mista's men. Others lay on the blood and rush-covered floor. The one object they all seemed to have in common, including Tiernan, was they all watched Mista and Erik.

Mista raked a crimson-streaked hand across her face as she stared at Erik.

"You are mistaken, my da would never have agreed to my marrying you. My duty is to my people— something you would not understand. Your lands lie fallow. You steal or buy grain to feed your household instead of treating your people, your warriors included, with respect. And that is why I would never marry you. I will not allow you to destroy my clan."

"And just how do you think to stop me, Mista?" Erik advanced closer.

"By killing you." Mista's words were soft, hiding the rage simmering beneath her skin. He had tormented her for the last few years. Always hitting where it hurt—trying to starve her clan in an effort to make her join with him in marriage.

"It would take a better warrior than you to do that. Why do you not allow one of your warriors to fight me? 'Twould be more fitting for a man to fight a man, than for me to fight a woman." His sneer increased as he continued. "There be better ways to deal with a female like you."

"I prefer to fight you myself, Erik. So, if you be finished talking, I suggest you prepare for your journey to Valhalla. Providing they will take a man whose soul is as black as yours." Mista watched and waited and then smiled when Erik's countenance changed to one of rage.

He would be much easier to defeat if he allowed his emotions to control him. She received no warning before he charged. Mista sidestepped, and then turned to face Erik. His features resembled a child denied their plaything. His green eyes gleamed with fury and the dip below his left eye began to pulse.

Yes. She needed him to lose control.

"What is wrong, Erik? Not as easy as you thought it would be?" She smiled and waited for him to make the next move. A bellow blasted her ears as he rushed her again. Mista held her ground. When he was mere inches away, she sliced down with her blade and a streak of red scored his chest. Not deep enough to kill him, but enough to make him yell in pain.

Before the cry finished echoing she carved a sliver into his left thigh.

"Arrh," Erik bellowed again and fell to his knees, but then with almost superhuman strength he rallied.

His steps were not as sure, nor strong, but he used his sword arm to attack with a fever of intensity that shocked Mista.

She brought her sword up to clash with his—on the defensive now. The blows caused a flash of pain to shoot from her wrist all the way to her shoulder. Before she could recover from one blow he struck again. Mista staggered backward, but kept her footing.

Cries of Erik's men did not overshadow the gasps of her own. She dare not look toward Tiernan. The look on his face would interfere with her emotions, and that is something she did not need. She must fight this battle alone.

Slowly but consistently she once again began to land offensive blows. Blood continued to drip onto the floor, and Erik's movements became disjointed. He swung his weapon but without any strength behind the blow.

In that moment, Mista changed her mind about killing him, although she might regret it. 'Twould be much better for both their clans if they could come to some type of understanding.

Erik stumbled and went down again. His head bowed toward the floor.

"Erik, lay down your weapon, and let us to come to an understanding that will benefit all our people."

When he raised his head, and his gaze looked to be filled with hope, she took but a moment to crush it.

"Nay, not by marriage, but by friendship. It is something our ancestors upheld for centuries. Surely we can find some common ground?" She held her breath and waited.

His sword clattered to the floor, and Mista allowed

herself an exhalation of relief. Only then did she permit her gaze to touch on those who stood battered, beaten down, and relieved.

Baldr inclined his head toward her, and Tiernan smiled, but his gaze was filled with concern. Only a few marks marred his tanned forearms, and she was thankful that not even the slightest scratch disturbed his handsome features.

Mista wanted this over and done with. She wanted to lie in Tiernan's arms, have him make love to her, and then just maybe she could convince him to spend the rest of *her* life here.

"Hear me well, you of Clan Runolfsson. I offer you a chance to leave here without reprisal, but you must swear an oath of allegiance that will only be broken by your death. An oath that from this night onward our clans will stand in friendship." She looked down at Erik.

"There is no need for further bloodshed or death for either of our people. We can be united against enemies that would do either of our clans harm."

Erik's men, who still held their weapons, laid them at their feet. One by one they dropped to one knee and bowed their heads toward Mista. For her that was more than enough. Most men, especially Vikings, would only go so far to humble themselves.

"Thank you. When we are finished here, your wounds will be cleaned, your dead sent to Valhalla in a blaze of glory, and you can return to your loved ones."

Mista focused her gaze on Erik. The man looked devastated, and she prayed he would do as his men had.

"Very well, Mista." He too bowed his head.

Her joy and relief were boundless. No more days

and nights of worrying when Erik would strike to taunt her men, steal her livestock, or burn her crops. No more worrying if he would be successful in kidnapping and forcing Mista to wed him.

"Thank you, Erik." She motioned for Baldr and Olav to come forward. Although her nemesis had accepted her terms, until he was off her land she would rather he be guarded—even if it were in the guise of help.

Her warriors reached down to help him to his feet, and Mista turned to go back to Tiernan.

"Mista?" Erik's voice pulled her back.

"Yes, Erik?" She waited to see what he might say.

Before she could react, Erik grabbed his discarded sword and rose from the floor in almost one motion. He thrust the weapon forward—straight into Mista's belly.

The gut-wrenching pain stole her breath. Her hand encircled the blade, her mouth open in shock, but she could not pull the blade free. Her hands were slick with blood.

"NO!" Tiernan's cry was the last thing she heard before falling into a void of darkness.

Chapter Seventeen

Willamina arrived back in the castle mere seconds ahead of the council and Catriona. She held the orb close to her breast, and did not plan on letting it go.

Catriona marched up to her, and held out her hand. "I believe you have something that belongs to the council."

"The Judgment Orb belongs to the king, or the queen if the king is not available." Willamina purred the words.

"Just so, but since I am of royal blood, and you are not, then I will be taking possession of the orb." Catriona's words invoked the rage and fear, previously banked down, to surge to the surface. She should have been more careful. She should have waited to retrieve the orb. But still the battle was not lost. She would use it as she planned.

Willamina thrust the orb forward just as a blast of magick rocked the castle. The commingled crimson, black, and purple streams threw all of them into shock, and in her case panic.

Tiernan!

"Da. It's coming from him." Catriona at first looked overjoyed, and then her brows creased into a frown. "Something is wrong."

Before Willamina could use the orb to incapacitate Tiernan's whelp or the male fae, Catriona grabbed her arm and snatched it from her.

"Bring her! We will follow my da's trail of magick and then find out just what damage this witch has done."

****

Tiernan sat on the floor, his arms around Mista, her blood soaking into his pants and tunic. Her skin pale as an alabaster moon, and her lips and eyelids had taken on a cool blue tinge.

The floor around him was awash with crimson, and the wound in her belly gaped, still pumping out her life essence.

Mista was dying.

His magick had failed him.

When Erik struck his blow, Tiernan did not panic. He knew what he would be giving up to heal Mista, and it would be worth it, but nothing had helped. Enraged he'd wanted to cleave Erik's head from his body, but that right had been denied him when Baldr did the honor.

Now he sat, holding the most precious being in his life—except for his daughters. His chest hurt as he waited for Mista to take her final breath. What good was magick if he could not save the one he loved?

He pressed his thumb to her lips, the soft flesh even cooler to his touch. Tiernan leaned forward to taste her lips one last time when gasps erupted around him. He looked up to see columns of sparkles, five in all, coalesced inside the hall.

"Da!" Catriona's cry was a welcome balm to his shattered soul, but the addition of all four of the council members did not touch him. Yes, he would lose his powers, his birthright, and his status as king.

But nothing mattered to losing Mista.

"Catriona…" His voice trailed off as she moved to his side and stared down at Mista.

"What happened?" Her question reawakened the rage that had fled with the onset of his despair.

"She is what happened!" Tiernan pointed at Willamina, and his daughter as well as Jared, Alex, and Gideon all looked at the fae.

"Da, what did she do?" Catriona's tone was soft, and in his heart, he knew she wanted to know everything, but he needed to be with Mista.

"It can wait. Mista is dying."

"Who is she?" Alex asked. Tiernan spared him but a glance below allowing his gaze to return to Mista's face.

"She is my heart. And she is dying. I can't save…" His words broke off as Mista's frame shuddered, and his own body shivered with desperation.

"Help me save her, please!"

"No!" Willamina's denial caused a chorus of snarls from Mista's people, but none as potent as Tiernan's.

"I say this is the time to change some of those rules, uncles." Catriona looked toward the fae Tiernan had called friends and family for several millennia.

"I agree." Alex knelt at Tiernan's side, followed by Gideon and Catriona. Jared still maintained the grip he had on Willamina.

"You can't help him. It is wrong. Against our rules," Willamina screamed.

"And since my da helped write those rules, they can be changed. Now shut up, Willamina, before I turn you into a ferret." Catriona's threat had the desired effect. Willamina pursed her lips but did not utter another word.

"Perhaps together, we can help your woman, Tiernan." Gideon placed his hand over the one Tiernan held against Mista's wound. Alex followed as did Catriona. With their eyes closed they pressed into the now barely seeping wound. If this did not work then he would lose her forever.

The room began to spin around Tiernan. Rainbow colors swirled against his closed lids. He pressed harder against Mista's belly. Dare he hope their combined magick would work?

His palm started to burn, the fire coating it growing hotter—more intense. But more than that, he could feel Mista's essence, which had been almost non-existent, growing stronger.

He opened his eyes and watched as her lids begin to twitch, and then open. The look of shock in her blue gaze was welcome. She was conscious.

Mista looked up at him, and then around in wonder. Finally she spoke. "Tiernan, what happened?"

"Oh, my love. Erik stabbed you, and you were dying."

Her gaze turned pensive. "I remember, but I don't understand. How can I have been dying, but now I feel fine?"

Tiernan laughed with joy as he and the others moved their hands away from Mista's flesh.

"Son of Thor. Her wound's healed." Baldr's gasp was echoed by the other warriors.

"Daughter of a faery would be more correct, Baldr, my friend. Without Catriona's help, as well as my friends, she would have died."

Mista stirred in his arms, and he helped her stand

haltingly to her feet. "So this is your daughter?"

"Yes, my eldest." Tiernan's tone was edged in pride as it should be in Mista's opinion. The woman now standing at his side was beautiful.

"Thank you all for your help." Mista reached out to have her hand taken and squeezed by Catriona and the two men.

Her world was a bit off-kilter. She remembered the pain of Erik's sword but then nothing except for a bright light that grew closer as her body grew weaker. Aye, she was indeed grateful for the healing they had wrought, but some part of Mista knew they had help from a higher power. For she had glimpsed a beautiful world way beyond even the realm Tiernan came from.

"Mista, child, I…" Baldr's gruff tones preceded the bone crunching hug he gave her. She hugged him back before speaking, "Enough, Baldr, you are crushing me."

His roar of laughter started an avalanche of hugs as Gunhilde sped from the back of the hall from where she'd guarded the women and servants. The night grew into day before Mista was able to go to the one she wanted to be hugged by.

Tiernan had been just as busy as Mista—greeting his daughter and friends, as well as speaking with another man who looked to be guarding the tall, dark-haired woman. The woman she assumed to be Willamina looked anything but pleased.

Mista had sent the men who'd sworn allegiance to her back home, and they took with them Erik's body. Hopefully, the one they chose to take his place would honor the new alliance. If not then they would fight again. The wounded were being seen to, and Gunhilde had bustled to the kitchen to see about substance for

Mista, Tiernan, and their guests.

"My love, you should be resting." Tiernan's arms slid around her waist, and she leaned back against his broad chest.

"I am fine, Tiernan, but I do feel the need of a bath." She turned in his embrace and reached up to caress his face. "Would you please entertain your daughter and friends until I return?"

"I'd much rather help you." His whisper and the look in his eyes had her almost agreeing. But she needed time to scrub away the blood and the memories of the last several hours. Mista also needed time to think. Whether Tiernan realized it or not, he would be returning to his homeland. And she needed to shore up her defenses against his leaving.

"Nay, I think 'twould be best if I took care of that chore alone. You would only distract me." The smile she gave him did not quite reach her heart.

"Whatever you wish, but I will see you to your chamber."

She nodded her head and they left the hall. Tiernan did not touch Mista as they made their way up the stairs and then trod the corridor to her chamber. She opened the door to the wonderful sight of a tub already filled with steaming water. Thankful for Gunhilde's foresight, she allowed her body to slump. Although the grievous wound was gone, she still felt the leavings of having done battle.

"Thank you, Tiernan. I will try not to be long." She hoped her words would send him from the room, but instead, he took her into his arms. She tried to step back, but he would have none of her evasive tactics.

Mista tried harder, she did not think she could

146

stand Tiernan making love to her again. For she knew he would want to complete the act, but if he did, then she would never have the strength to give him up.

"Mista, I will not make love to you at this moment. I want you well-rested when I do."

Although it felt as if a hundred knives sharper than Erik's blade raked her insides Mista did what she had to. "Tiernan, I would prefer you do not make love to me at all."

"Why?" His stark and agonized tone did nothing to vanquish the pain.

"Because, you will be leaving, and I would like for you to go as soon as possible after breaking your fast." Her words sounded harsh, but it was nothing compared to the heartache riding her soul.

"Mista, I don't want to leave you. I want you as my wife." Tiernan's words shattered her heart, and chipped away at her resolve."

"Nay, you have to go back to your kingdom. Look at what happened while you were gone." Mista had only heard bits and pieces while in the hall, but enough to know Willamina would be a force Tiernan would have to reckon with if she was not watched.

"Willamina will be dealt with, never fear."

"But you still have to face additional punishment for using your magick to heal me." She hated she would be the cause of Tiernan losing his powers forever.

"No, I will not." At her questioning look, he continued. "My magick will remain with me. The council, with no persuasion, has decided Willamina's punishment was unwarranted for the crime I committed."

Her sigh of relief coincided with him taking her

into his arms once more. "Now, let's talk about why you cannot marry me."

"Tiernan, 'tisn't just you having to leave, but the fact I cannot. We have discussed this before. There is no one to take my place as chieftain."

"What if there were? Would you marry me then?"

"You know very well the only rightful heir would have been my brother. Baldr, who would be up to the task, and would do so if I asked him, would rather be in charge of the warriors. And now with this alliance in place with the Runolfsson clan, I cannot take the chance that another chieftain might not keep the agreement in tact."

She walked away to look out the window. The day was bright with sunshine—strange since her heart felt as if the entire world was encased in darkness.

"Do you love me?" His question only drove the knives in harder.

"How can you ask me that? Of course I do."

"Then I see no problem. We will marry and you will return to court with me." Tiernan's obstinacy almost scared a smile out of Mista, but then all amusement fled. He had to understand—she could not marry him. Not now, possibly never.

Chapter Eighteen

Tiernan wanted to hit something or somebody. Right now, he did not care who or what. Mista, the stubborn woman, refused to listen to reason. Her aloof but firm, "Please go now," agitated him to no end. What would it take to get her to change her mind?

"Da, are you okay?" Catriona sat down next to him at the table, and then poured them both a goblet of mead. She waited and when he remained silent, she took a sip.

"Ooh. We need this recipe. It's almost as good as our ambrosia." She smiled at Tiernan.

He knew what she was trying to do, but it was not working. But this was his child, and he would try to play it her way.

"I agree. The mead here is excellent. Now, how is your husband, and also how did you find out something was wrong?"

"Derek is just fine, Da. He's out on maneuvers, and let's just say after a week or more of not having you send me mind thoughts on whether or not I planned to make you a grandfather, I became concerned." She picked up her glass again, and Tiernan did the same.

"It didn't take long after seeing Willamina, the witch, installed on your throne that I went to talk to the uncles. All they remember is missing the meeting. And they were told you were visiting me. And I was told you were having a romantic interlude." Catriona's nose crinkled.

"You know me better than that, and I thank you for your help. But I guess you've realized I have found love once more." He wasn't sure how Catriona would feel about him falling in love.

"Yes, I did surmise that after witnessing your magickal sparks all the way to the castle. And the look on your face said it all." She picked up her goblet. "So, can I assume there will be a queen in residence?"

"Would it bother you if there were?" He hoped not, but if Mista would marry him, then he would do what he must to have her always at his side.

"Of course not. You can thank Derek for that." At his confused look, Catriona continued. "Before falling in love with Derek, I would have been devastated, but Da, you deserve to have someone who loves you. And I assume Mista does?"

"Yes, but she refuses to marry me." Tiernan hated to admit that to his daughter, but she was more than old enough to understand. No longer was she a spoiled princess. Her maturity since involving herself with mortals, as well as helping Derek's sister find her love—not to mention loving a mortal herself had grown into that of a woman who knew the pitfalls a relationship could bring.

"Why?" She caught his hand and squeezed it, and he squeezed hers in return.

"Mista has been the chieftain of her clan for the last several years since she lost her father. She is the only heir, and she won't leave her duty."

"She is an only child?"

"No, but her brother was abducted before Mista

was born. They never found him nor did they find a body. I believe deep in her heart, she hopes he survived."

Tiernan looked around the hall, wishing Mista would put in an appearance. Time was passing, and he did not want to sentence Willamina without her being there. The fae's actions had almost caused Mista her life.

"What if he is alive, would he even want to come back after all this time?" Catriona's question made Tiernan think.

Vidar would probably feel like a fae without wings. But how could he convince Mista of this? What could he do to help her be in control of her clan but still be his wife?

"I don't know, Cat, but the possibility of him being alive and not making his way back are pretty non-existent in my opinion."

"Well, I can help search for him, and if you could convince Mista to marry you, then why can't she be with her clan during the day and then with you at night?" Catriona raised an eyebrow. "It works for Raven and Wulfgar, and with me and Derek."

Tiernan mulled her words over in his mind. It would work for him also, if only Mista would agree.

"Would you like for me to talk to her?" Catriona's gaze was hopeful. Maybe it wouldn't hurt to have a woman talk to Mista.

"Yes, thank you. You are a good daughter, and I love…" His words faded away as he spied Mista entering the room. She was dressed in a long gown the color of her eyes, and although she looked tired, she did look more relaxed.

Maybe with him being able to use his magick again, since the council had demolished Willamina's previous punishment, he could make things easier for Mista—even if she would not consent to be his wife.

She made her way to the table and took a seat on the other side of Tiernan. "Good evening, Tiernan, Princess Catriona."

"Please call me Cat." Catriona reached past Tiernan and caught Mista's hand in hers. "It is an honor to meet someone who has completely captivated my da."

Heat caressed Mista's face at Tiernan's daughter's words. She wasn't quite certain what to say in response.

"Mista, I have no secrets from Cat. I told her I love you, and want to marry you." He touched her face, and Mista wanted to melt into his caress.

"Thank you, Cat. I…I am glad you are here." Mista accepted the goblet Tiernan handed her. "It is good that you have come. Your father missed you."

"And I him. Now, let's talk about why you can't marry him."

Mista strangled on her mead. After being pounded on the back by Tiernan, she finally got her breath back.

"I really do not think 'tis the time to—"

"Oh but it is, Mista. I know that all that has happened has been devastating to you. How could it not be, but trust me when I say, there is a way for you two to be together, and you still be able to take care of your clan." Catriona sounded so certain, Mista wondered if something could be worked out.

"How is that possible?" She allowed the cuffs of her gown to slide over her hands to hide their trembling.

"Well, you know my husband is also mortal and has to be gone for several weeks at a time. I divide my time without him at the Seelie Court with my da, and at mine and Derek's home."

"Tiernan told me your husband is a mortal. How can you do that?"

Catriona looked at Tiernan. "Well…let's just say he is an extraordinary husband. As to how it is possible, that's easy. I know you have not seen magick, since da could not use his without reprisals, but it's a simple matter of just teleporting…" At Mista's confused look, Catriona explained.

"Moving from one place to another without having to travel by ordinary means." Catriona stood up. "Why don't I show you what I'm talking about?"

Mista watched as Catriona stood there, and then she disappeared—to reappear across the room. She looked around but no one else seemed to be shocked. In fact it was as if Catriona was invisible to them.

A second later, Catriona sat next to Mista once again.

"How did you do this without the others seeing?"

"Simple. I used a cloaking spell so only you could see me," Catriona answered.

"And you…you can do this?" Mista looked at Tiernan.

"Yes, and more. But Cat is good, very good." Tiernan's smile was a blend of parental pride and love.

"Truly? And how would this tel-e-portion work with us?"

"Come," Tiernan took her hand and gently pulled her to her feet. "Allow me to demonstrate."

His arms encircled her waist, and Mista felt the

walls around her fade away. When she opened her eyes she stood inside a building that was wondrously decorated in gold, but the red she could have done without. It reminded her too much of death and blood.

"Is this your home?" Her question came out in a bit of a squeak.

"Yes, but I see Willamina has decided to change things around." Tiernan waved his hand, and the crimson was replaced with a deep purple.

"I like this better." Mista smiled at him, and took a step forward. Her legs were shaky but there did not seem to be any other ill effects of having travel miles and worlds away from her home.

"I'm glad, but you know you can do whatever you want to make this your home." Tiernan moved to sit in the throne like chair on a raised dais.

"Now come, sit." He motioned to a chair similar to his.

Mista walked up the two steps and seated herself gingerly on the edge of the seat. "Your home is lovely, Tiernan, but what are we doing here?"

"I wanted to prove to you how simple it would be to travel back and forth. I can be with you most of the time, and we can spend the nights here or at your home." Tiernan knew he sounded a bit desperate, but fae's wings, he wanted this to work.

"And what happens if I stay here at night or any other time, and I'm needed at home?" Her question gave him hope. At least she wasn't tossing out the entire idea.

"Baldr will call you. He knows as do most of your people now what I am."

"But how can he call from such a distance?"

"I will give him a special armband that will enable Baldr to speak directly to either you or myself."

"And this would work?" Mista's eyes were open even wider than they had been upon arriving at his home.

"Yes, watch this." Tiernan winked at her. "Catriona, have your uncles arrived in the hall?" The men on the council had been securing Willamina in the dungeon Tiernan had previously known up close and personal.

"Yes, Da, they are awaiting your return." His daughter laughed. "And I hope you will have good news for us."

"We will return shortly." Tiernan grinned at Mista.

"But you didn't use an armband to call Cat." Her gaze was a brilliant blue, and her lips parted in a pink oval.

"Well, I have years of experience, and being able to use my magick is a bonus when it comes to long-distance conversations."

Mista turned her head slightly, and her profile was a thing of beauty to Tiernan. Just having her here with him made his heart soar beyond the universe. Her pensive look, however, made his stomach ached with anxiety.

"Should we not get back?"

He pulled himself away from his thoughts. "Yes, but first…"

Tiernan stood up and then moved to kneel at Mista's feet. "I will only ask you this once more. If you don't say yes now, then I don't think you ever will."

He pulled breath into his lungs and then spoke. "Mista, will you marry me?" Tiernan held his breath

155

and kept his eyes on her face. He feared he'd lost his battle to convince her when she looked away from him.

"Will your people allow a marriage between us?" Her question was good one, but Tiernan had the approval of the council and for the most part the fae in his kingdom would be happy if he was happy.

"Yes. Now what is your answer?" His words were abrupt, and he expected Mista to take umbrage at his tone.

"I say yes, Tiernan, King of the Seelie Court."

"You will?" Shock was overridden by a joy that took his breath.

"Yes, but on one condition. No, make that two." His elation came to a crashing halt.

"What are these conditions?"

"First, I want to be able to practice with my sword when I'm here, and"—Mista turned a look of pure devilment on Tiernan—"second, I want a crown like that one." She pointed to Tiernan's court crown, encased in a glass display.

"You shall have both." He leapt to his feet and pulled her into his arms. "But maybe we could start out with a slightly smaller version of court-wear."

He wished himself into more suitable clothing for his status, and Mista's eyes almost popped out of her head as she gave him a long slow look. He hoped she liked his black garb, and the purple cape he wore slung back over his shoulders. Bands of amethyst and gold, more elaborate than the previous ones, now rode his forearms, and the gold circlet he preferred rested on his head.

"Yes, I do like the version you are wearing." Mista whispered the words. By the blush on her cheeks, he knew she wasn't talking primarily about the crown.

"And I prefer us both to be naked as soon as possible." He gazed down into her eyes and then caught her lips with his own to steal a kiss that left him wanting much more.

When he could pull back, he did. "For now"—he brushed a finger over her blush-kissed face—"we need to get Willamina sentenced and get married." He ran a hand down the curve of her hip. "For the next time I have you in bed, I will not be stopping for any reason."

"And I will not be asking you to," Mista whispered.

Chapter Nineteen

Time must run differently in their diverse worlds Mista thought. Whereas it seemed only minutes had passed since she and Tiernan had gone to and returned from his home, in actuality it had been a couple of hours.

The afternoon was waning, and it would soon be time for their evening meal. But first Tiernan would judge the woman who had sent him on a journey that could have killed him.

The great hall had been cleared of all but Mista, Tiernan, his daughter, Baldr, the other fae men, and of course Willamina.

The witch, as Tiernan called her, stood motionless. Her form encased in red silk, her raven hair falling almost to her hips, and her green eyes flashed with what could only be malice. Mista hoped that the men would be able to contain Willamina. If they could not then she worried for all their safety.

"Willamina, you have defied the laws of our court. You have also used your own jealousy to punish our king when it was not your right to do so. And you took what did not belong to you." Alex held up a slim metal object with a glass ball on the end.

Mista looked at the men who stood by the dark-haired fae's side. Both Jared with chestnut hair and Gideon with a silver mane remained motionless, but she was certain if Willamina even twitched they would weave magick that would cover the entire hall.

"Now you will be sentenced for these crimes by the one you have wronged." A shudder crept up Mista's spine at the caress of doom in Alex's baritone.

Tiernan's stride was that of a warrior king. His broad shoulders, expansive chest, hard butt, and long legs were fluid sensuality. Mista could watch him walk for hours without getting tired, but she would much rather be in bed with him. Soon she would be, and he would finally be hers for next to forever.

Tiernan stopped before the witch. "Willamina." His voice pulled Mista out of her lustful thoughts and back to the proceedings at hand.

"You purposely tried to do me harm, and for that reason I would have every right to ask for your life in return." He leaned in closer. "The fact that you also placed Mista in danger—almost causing her death—warrants a punishment more severe than just taking your life."

"Seriously, Tiernan, I hardly think a *mortal* is worth so much trouble." Willamina's acidic tone caused Mista to pull back in her chair. The occupants of the hall gaped as Tiernan's face went from royally incensed to stone. Even knowing he would never hurt *her*, Mista still feared the consequences of Willamina's words.

"*This mortal* is the woman I love, who will be your queen in a matter of hours, and—"

"Queen? You would go so far as to marry this Viking? To give her a place of honor at your side? To help rule our people?" Willamina's countenance changed from derision to fury. "How dare you allow her to have a say in our court. She is nothing but a—"

159

"Silence! I have heard all I want to hear from you. Now, you will listen to *me*." Tiernan took the object Alex held out to him.

"The council, minus your vote, has accepted Mista as their queen. My daughter, who has had the acceptance to rule on the council if another member was absent, has also given her approval. You no longer have anything to say, Willamina."

Mista's soon-to-be-husband held the silver orb aloft and then spoke again. "As of this moment, Willamina, you are stripped of all your magical powers."

"NOOOOOOO!" Her shriek was ignored.

"And, you will be forbidden to collect even the least of the possessions you own." The orb began to swirl with a combination of colors. Mista sat on the edge of the bench.

"You are hereby vanished to the outer rim of the universe. To the Realm of Despair."

Willamina dropped to her knees and began to weep. The tears looked genuine. Mista leaned over to Catriona.

"What is this realm?"

Catriona's smile wasn't at all nice. "It is a place where those who have no hope congregate. It's like a last resort for those whose souls seem to have no recourse but to weep in despair."

"Can they never leave?"

"Not without summoning a member of the council to intervene. That is the purpose of being there. Some are sent; some choose to go." Catriona turned her gaze back toward her da and Willamina.

The image Cat invoked stirred compassion and

sorrow in Mista's heart. To be so despairing of hope they would allow themselves to be possibly incarcerated forever.

"Please, Tiernan, not that. I promise I will behave."

Mista was of a mind to believe the woman, but Tiernan looked more than a bit skeptical.

"You have lied, stolen, and given little regard to what would happen to those you malign. You, Willamina, have also disregarded what would happen if you were caught." Tiernan's gaze turned an icy blue.

"Did you truly think you could get away with this? To what purpose, Willamina? Sooner or later someone, and in this case Catriona, realized something was wrong. If you did it on the spur of the moment, I could relate it to emotional turmoil, but all your actions smack of premeditation. I don't believe you will change."

The colors grew stronger, almost malevolent in the intensity of purple stirring the air. The floor where Willamina knelt swirled with movement. The rushes beneath her knees wavered as if they were there one moment and then gone the next. A low hum penetrated the room, and the room shook slightly with vibration. The floor beneath Mista's feet pulsated.

She glanced at Catriona, but saw no alarm on her face. In fact, the fae looked pleased.

"No, Tiernan…" Willamina's words disappeared, as her body seemed to cave in on itself. Then she was gone.

Tiernan shook hands with his fellow council members, before returning to the table. His expression was pensive and possibly a bit regretful. Mista ran her hand down his arm, and the muscle beneath her palm jumped.

"Be you all right?" She clutched his hand when he grasped the one she still held on his forearm.

"Yes. I don't like what I had to do but without punishment for those who defy our laws, we would have a world where chaos rules. Not to mention those weaker would suffer—mortals and immortals alike."

"I know. Making decisions is not always easy." Judging disputes among her clan could be heartbreaking at times, but nothing like what Tiernan had just endured.

"No, but let's forget about unpleasantness for now. I believe we have a wedding to attend." The smile he sent her highlighted a gaze that contained a bit of lust, a whole lot of caring, and more than enough love.

Mista stood up and then stopped. "But we've made no plans for a wedding, or for the feast to follow."

"Mista, allow me to handle those details for you." Catriona grinned. "We can have the wedding tomorrow morning, then a midday feast. And if you and Da agree we can have a reception at the castle."

"Tiernan?"

"Whatever you want, Mista. But the quicker we are wed the happier I will be." He pulled her in close and then captured her lips. Her breath hitched for a moment at the rich, sensual taste of his open mouth kiss. When he deepened the caress she melted into his embrace. She would have stayed there forever but someone cleared their throat.

"Mista, I would be honored to give you away." Baldr's gruff tone belied the smile on his lips.

"And I would like nothing more. You are like a father to me, Baldr. So let us celebrate with some mead, and I will tell you how you and I will handle the affairs of our clan when I'm not here."

****

Dawn was not far off, and Mista was wide-awake. The attack within Einarsson walls, Erik's fight to the death, her near-death experience, and then Tiernan's healing her weighed on her mind. Not to mention the take-charge attitude of his daughter in regards to the wedding preparations. Before Catriona was halfway through her recital of what to have for the feast, the reception at the Seelie Court, and the wedding, Mista's eyelids closed and her mind shut down as she dropped into sleep.

She barely remembered being carried from the hall, but she did cherish the kiss Tiernan dropped on her mouth after tucking her into bed. Yet, in a way being carried around like a child when she was a chieftain was a bit demoralizing and embarrassing. But at least most of her warriors had already been enjoying the snores of blissful sleep.

Perhaps she should get up. The wedding would be held around four hours after sunrise, and that time would be here before she…was ready.

Her feelings of turmoil had nothing to do with her future husband as much as it did with being a queen to his people. Mista wasn't quite certain she could handle the duties of royalty.

Chapter Twenty

Tiernan drained the third cup of ambrosia he'd been handed in the short time he and Mista had arrived at his home. Catriona had outdone herself with a festive scene very much like the one he'd magicked up weeks prior. His new bride, however, had looked dazed, but then she had every right to. Her life had been turned every which way it could since he'd fallen into it.

She'd been a vision of seductive innocence at their mortal wedding, although he knew she would hate to be thought of as anything but tough. He'd looked deeper beyond the soft smile she'd given him, and found just a bit of fear, as well as apprehension.

Tiernan hoped it was just wedding jitters. Even though his wife was an extraordinary warrior and just leader for her clan, Mista was still a woman. It could be she had reservations about the night to come. Reservations he would eradicate when she returned.

Catriona had spirited her away to find something a bit more in sync with what the other fae women wore. Tiernan would have been content in gazing on Mista in her royal-blue wedding apparel, but undoubtedly Cat picked up on something he hadn't.

Women could be complicated at times, and Mista…well…

A collected tide of gasps echoed around Tiernan. He looked up and found acquaintances, fae who

164

frequented the court when he was there, and Alex, Jared, and Gideon along with their wives staring toward the family quarters.

With his vision obscured by well-wishers, Tiernan stood up at the same moment the throng parted. Mista as he'd never imagined walked with her head erect, her carriage that of a chieftain, and now his queen.

The glitter of lights strung from the ceiling paled in comparison to the sparks of sapphire glowing back at him from her eyes as she walked toward the throne dais. The royal purple of her gown complimented his armbands, and hugged her curves in a way that made him want to rip the gown off and take her to bed.

His shaft hardened with the thought of having Mista naked beneath him, but he willed the lust away. There was one more thing he needed to do before he could make her his.

Amethysts and diamonds in dangling clusters and ropes of jewels adorned Mista's earlobes and neck. Her bare arms carried the signature and matching smaller armbands of her new status. She walked with grace and dignity—never showing to the fae around her by even the minute gesture or glance that she might be frightened of all the strangeness encompassing her.

Catriona followed behind Mista, her gown a glorious red and her wrists decked out in armbands to match. She carried a satin pillow with a scaled down version of Tiernan's crown. Once he placed the symbol of royalty on Mista's head, and accepted the congratulations of his peers, then he could escape with his bride to their chamber.

Mista gained the first step to the dais, and Tiernan reached out his hand to bring her up the last one and into his embrace. He placed a banked-down kiss on her lips, and then greeted Catriona.

"Well done, my daughter. Thank you."

"All in the twist of a wrist, Da. I am more than happy to do anything I can to make this transition easier on Mista." She graced her stepmother with a smile before mounting the last step to stand next to Tiernan.

"Thank you all for coming this evening, my friends. Most of you gathered here knew my late wife, Alisanne, and that I vowed I would never marry again." He tugged Mista closer. "But this woman changed my mind. By now you all know about Willamina, but the one bright spot in what she did is I found Mista. She is the chieftain of her clan on mortal earth, and will continue to govern her people."

A few of those gathered looked a bit shocked, but not appalled, at the fact Mista was mortal.

Tiernan stepped back from Mista, lifted the crown, and held it aloft. "Make welcome the new queen of our Seelie Court, Mista." He grinned down at her frozen expression, placed the jewel-and-gold accoutrement on top of Mista's upswept hair. He leaned forward and allowed himself a second of bliss as he caressed the lobe of her ear before whispering. "You are doing great. They will love you as do I."

Drawing back Tiernan witnessed the flash of white in her otherwise still face. The loveliness of her smile brought warmth to his heart, and a reminder that in just a matter of time they would be away from the celebration. He hoped Mista could hang in there for that long.

Mista smiled until every muscle in her face hurt. She wasn't certain but felt that if she had to shake hands or accept hugs from Tiernan's friends one more time she just might fall on her face. She'd lost count after the first fifty or so people passed through what Tiernan called a receiving line. Now the hour grew even later, and the line still seemed to swell.

"Mista, are you okay?" Catriona's soft query prompted a genuine smile.

"Aye, just a bit tired." Mista shook hands with Jared and then watched as he and Tiernan clasped arms like warriors. It was good that his friends were here and supported him. She was happy they seemed to accept her, but the magnitude of responsibility in being Tiernan's wife still made her want to break out in a rash of hives.

"If you want to sit down for a while, I'm sure no one would mind."

"Nay, I will be fine." She whispered back to Catriona, and with mixed feelings prayed the time would pass quickly and then…

Tiernan watched the interchange between his wife and daughter. He knew Mista was almost out on her feet. It was time to put an end to the festivities, at least for him and his new bride.

"Jared, we are ducking out now. Can you, Alex, and Gideon handle the rest?"

"We can, and I'm sure Catriona will be around for a while won't you?" Jared turned to Cat.

"Yes, go Da. You deserve the time off." She gave him a hug, and gave Mista one also. "I'll see you in a couple of days. I'll bring Derek up to meet you. Don't worry about a thing. I'll pop in to see Baldr also."

"A couple of days? I was planning to go back tomorrow to check on my people." Mista sounded confused and Tiernan bit back a grin before scooping her up into his arms.

"Sorry, love, but you will be much too busy for the next few days to check on anything." Her sweet open-mouthed astonishment pulled Tiernan in like a man dying of thirst. He couldn't wait to quench his need with Mista.

****

The moment the chamber door closed, he braced Mista's body against the gold-plated surface so he could free his hands. His palms cupped her face. He ran a finger down her elegant cheekbones, and then traced his thumb over her bottom lip.

"Mista, do you realize even one tenth of how much I want you?" His whisper fell at her neck as he licked and suckled the slim column.

"Nay, but I do know I want you." Her words were just a breath of air but enough to harden his shaft even more. He rejoiced in her answer, but why was she still so tense? She might act like a woman who wanted a man, but beneath the soft contours of skin, her heart beat so erratically he wondered if indeed the thought of the coming night frightened her.

"Are you certain?"

Mista jerked her head up and looked him straight in the eyes. "Aye, 'tis not the coming night so much as being a queen."

Relieved beyond imagination, Tiernan laughed, and Mista tried to escape the thigh he had wedged under her hips.

"Mista, I'm sorry. It's just I fear now that we are wed, and unless someone wants to be zapped with a bolt of magick we will not be interrupted, that you might be apprehensive."

"How could you think I be such a coward? If I have any timidity about tonight it is because, I be afraid I will disappoint you."

His jaw dropped, but when he realized her blue eyes held nothing but sincerity he closed his mouth. "Oh, love, you have nothing to worry about. Truth be known, I am a bit frightened I might not be as gentle as I should."

"Well, perhaps we could compromise." Mista sent him a smile that brightened the already glowing room lit by candles and firelight. "I promise if I decide I do not like gentle, I will let you know."

His arousal grew harder, and he turned her so she rode higher on his thigh—bringing her flush against his manhood. Her eyes widened but then she smiled once more.

The smile turned into a gasp when he slid his hand under her gown to touch warm and wet flesh.

"Tiernan?"

"Yes, my love?" His hands continued to caress her.

"I think we both have too many clothes on."

"I agree, wife." Tiernan spun away from the door, his arms full of a now-naked Mista. Her mouth opened in surprise and hopefully more than a bit of desire. He crossed the room to place her on the king-size bed. The purple satin sheets were a perfect foil for her creamy skin and hair. Her pulled her to the edge of the bed and leaned down to catch a ruched nipple between his lips.

Mista tasted of roses, ambrosia, and sensual woman. He ached to take her right then, but he wanted her to be ready for his possession.

Her head moved from side to side as he tongued, licked, and then lightly bit down on the succulent tip, while his left hand paid homage to her other breast. When both nipples were engorged, he began an exploration of her ribcage, her belly, and then the planes of her hips.

Tiernan felt as he'd implode from the inside. He needed this woman worse than he needed his magick. She was his magick, his life, his heart…

His fingers brushed the fringe of hair hiding her inner most treasure. Again he dipped into the slick heat. Mista whimpered, and he delved deeper. First one finger, then a second before he began to rotate them against the sides of her wet channel.

Her hips rose and gyrated against the digits holding her captive. Tiernan increased the pressure, and Mista moaned—a welcome sound. Soon he would take her.

Still caressing her inner core, he nuzzled the tops of her thighs with his lips, before lifting one leg and kissing the bend of her knee. Mista's movements escalated, her thighs clenched around his hand. When he felt her almost on the edge of falling over, he used magick to unclothe himself, and then eased his hand from her body.

"Tiernan!"

"Just a moment more, Mista." He grasped her delectable bottom, pulled her lower body off the bed, and she locked her legs around his waist. Her gaze resembled a blue, wave-drenched lake. Tiernan pressed the meteorite hardness of his arousal against the V of Mista's thighs.

"I will try to be gentle, Mista, but…"

"Tiernan, I am burning up with need."

He needed no other coercion and pushed himself forward. Although, technically she was no longer a virgin, her passage was tight. Sweat beaded on Tiernan's forehead as he tried to temper the urgency driving him to bury himself as deep as he could within her depths.

"So am I." His shaft burned but he bore the pain. Another inch, then another. Tiernan kept his pace slow until her hips began to rotate. Twisting, pushing, and meeting his thrusts head-on.

He drove harder, deeper. His body hummed, strung so tightly with lust he was almost out of his mind. He felt the inner spirals of heat lapping tighter and stronger.

Mista's eyes were glazed with desire, and he could feel the twin rush of heat building from her core. She was close. He wanted to fall with her.

Tiernan palmed her female flesh and found the engorged knob hidden between her nether lips. He pinched and tugged, all the while increasing his thrusts.

"Tiernan…" Her scream invaded the room, and a feral smile broke free. Now. Now was the time.

He moved harder, faster, deeper, and Mista came apart. Her body shook and flailed, and then in one short breath stiffened before she slumped back on the bed.

Tiernan's release came a second later. His insides imploded with a hundred asteroids. He managed to pull Mista's body all the way on the bed, then he lay next to her. The purple coverlet magically covered their love-beaded forms.

"I think I died." Mista spoke against his chest.

"Not possible. You're immortal now." Mista's head struck his chin, and Tiernan bit down on his tongue.

"What did you say?" She sat up in bed and gave him a stare that equaled the ones he'd received as her slave.

"There is no need to be upset. When we made love, my essence touched yours."

"And you think that makes me what... invincible?"

"No, but you will live for many millennia as my wife and queen." He tugged her back down, and tucked her next to his side.

"I do not understand. Catriona's husband is still a mortal, is he not? Why am I different?"

"Derek wished to remain mortal. If he ever decides differently then he will apply to the council for immortality status," Tiernan explained.

"But do I not have to do the same thing?"

"No, my love. As my wife and queen it is an automatic process. And you will be a good queen. Catriona will coach you, and I will be here to help." Tiernan placed a kiss against her slightly swollen lips.

"So, that is the price I pay for becoming your wife?" Her grin was mischievous, and he rejoiced in the fact that she no longer seemed fearful of assuming her royal duties.

"Yes, and if you don't like it, then I will have to find a suitable punishment for you." His hand found and then tweaked her nipple, but Mista stopped his attempted foray.

"Please do not talk about punishment. What Willamina did to you was wrong. You could have died." Mista's eyes held the glimmer of teardrops.

"Mista, I have a confession to make." Tiernan hugged her tightly.

"What is it?"

"The one thing I could not tell Willamina was she in a way did me a favor. Her idea of punishment led me to the only woman in my world or yours who could give me the one thing I didn't know I desired again—love."

Mista's sharp inhalation paved the way for another kiss that led to Tiernan making love to his wife for the second, then the third, and then the…

A word about the author...

Faith started her journey to publication when she joined the Romance board at iVillage.com, where she became a community leader. She has written book reviews for *Bridges* magazine, MyShelf.com and for *Romantic Times Book Reviews*. She also pens a column for a local magazine. Her dream of having her own work published is a blessing and an honor. Faith resides in the South with her daughter Amanda, memories of her now-angel husband Rick, and a special zoo crew of furry babies. Visit her at www.faithvsmith.com

Other books by Faith V. Smith:

Beware What You Wish
Kensington's Soul
Dunbar's Curse
Viking, Go Home
Semper Fi Magick
Gideon's Heart
Immortal Justice

Vidar Einarsson's life takes a paranormal turn when a former Special Ops buddy claims Vidar is from the past. He scoffs at his tale, but when whisked to an ancient Viking village, he soon realizes there is much in the world that is unexplained. His past and present come together to explode with mayhem, murder, and love as he finds his Viking Legacy.

Look for Vidar's story in *Vidar's Legacy*, coming soon from The Wild Rose Press.

Also available from The Wild Rose Press, Inc.

Immortal Justice by Faith V. Smith
http://amzn.com/B0057PNCRQ

Warrior Rogue by Nancy J. Cohen
http://amzn.com/B00AU62NQS

www.ingramcontent.com/pod-product-compliance
Lightning Source LLC
Chambersburg PA
CBHW072142170626
46813CB00004BA/1651